Trophy Kid

OR HOW I WAS ADOPTED BY THE

RICH AND FAMOUS

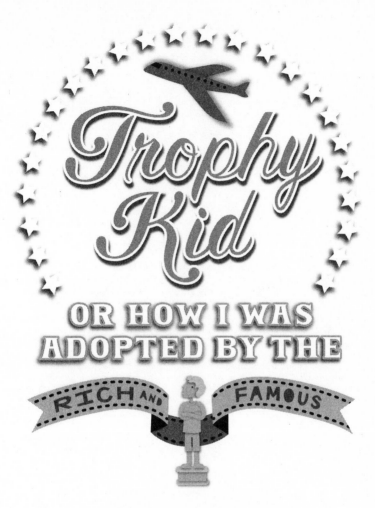

Trophy Kid

OR HOW I WAS ADOPTED BY THE

RICH AND FAMOUS

Steve Atinsky

delacorte press

Published by Delacorte Press
an imprint of Random House Children's Books
a division of Random House, Inc.
New York

This is a work of fiction. Names, characters, places, and incidents either
are the product of the author's imagination or are used fictitiously.
Any resemblance to actual persons, living or dead, events, or locales
is entirely coincidental.

Visit us on the Web! www.randomhouse.com/kids

Educators and librarians, for a variety of teaching tools, visit us at
www.randomhouse.com/teachers

Library of Congress Cataloging-in-Publication Data
Atinsky, Steve.
Trophy kid, or, How I was adopted by the rich and famous / Steve Atinsky. — 1st ed.
p. cm.
Summary: Since his much-publicized adoption at age three by American movie stars, thirteen-year-old
Josef's carefully scripted public life has hidden the isolation he feels at home, but writing a book with a
ghostwriter reveals much about his adoptive family and the one he lost during the war in Croatia.

ISBN 978-0-385-73049-5 (trade hc) — ISBN 978-0-385-90181-9 (glb)

[1. Family—Fiction. 2. Authorship—Fiction. 3. Orphans—Fiction. 4. Adoption—Fiction.
5. Celebrities—Fiction. 6. Family life—California—Fiction. 7. Croatian Americans—Fiction.
8. Bel Air (Los Angeles, Calif.)—Fiction. 9. Dubrovnik (Croatia)—Fiction. 10. Croatia—Fiction.]
I. Title. II. Title: Trophy kid. III. How I was adopted by the rich and famous.

PZ7.A8575Tro 2008
[Fic]—dc22
2007030270

The text of this book is set in 12-point Goudy.

Book design by Kenneth L. Holcomb

Printed in the United States of America

10 9 8 7 6 5 4 3 2 1

First Edition

Acknowledgments

Thanks to Marian Bodnar and Justin Rosenholtz for their helpful suggestions and encouragement after reading the first draft. Special thanks to my editor, Jodi Keller, whose magical red pen (actually it was a number two pencil) made a lot of unnecessary material disappear, and to my publisher, Beverly Horowitz, who believed I could write books for young readers.

prologue

I'm a trophy kid. You know, a status symbol. I haven't been in the news lately, but I'd be surprised if you haven't heard of me. My adoptive mother is America's Sweetheart and Academy Award–winning actress Greta Powell. My adoptive father is actor turned director, turned producer, turned international crusader for human rights, turned political candidate Robert Francis. Greta and Robert won me in a bidding war with eight other high-profile power couples and a few bachelor billionaires. I still hold the record for the most expensive adoption: $3.2 million.

It was in Dubrovnik, near the end of the war in Yugoslavia. I was three years old, holding the hand of my mother, walking to my sister's school, when several loud explosions went off around us. One of the blasts seemed to have come from where my sister's school was located. My mother pushed me into a doorway and told me to stay still. She said she would be back in a few minutes with my sister. I saw her disappear around a corner. The next moment there was an explosion on the block she had turned onto. I ran into the street after her. The shelling continued. Something small and sharp hit me just above my right eye and I started crying. Still I kept running after my mother. A Croatian soldier came into the street and picked me up. I screamed for my mother as he carried me to safety. It was all captured on camera and broadcast on news stations around the world.

I was taken to the nearest military facility. All I could tell the soldiers was my first name, Josef. They called me Joey. There was an exhaustive search to find the parents or any relatives of the little blond boy with blue eyes and newly sewn stitches over his right eyebrow, who had wandered into the street while missiles were exploding all around him.

Soldiers took turns playing with me and distracting me with ice cream and chocolates when I cried for my mother. All the while, the cameras rolled.

One morning, two Croatian soldiers took me to the neighborhood where I had been rescued. Several camera crews tagged along. The soldiers took me door to door, asking me, "Is this where you live?"

"No," I said over and over again—until we came to a green apartment building.

"Mommy!" I said excitedly, running up the inside stairs.

At the top was our apartment. I tried to open the door, but it was locked. One of the soldiers forced it open.

I ran from room to room looking for my mother. She wasn't there, of course. I didn't call out for my daddy. Only a few days before I ran into the street after my mother, she had told me that my father was in heaven and wouldn't be coming home. He had been an engineer in the army and had been killed when the Serbs blew up the bridge he was rebuilding. I've always liked the fact that my father was a soldier who built things rather than blew them apart.

After I'd searched every room, I started crying. One of the soldiers took my hand and led me out of the apartment. I took one look back, just in case my mother and sister had been playing hide-and-seek and were now going to surprise me by leaping out of a closet. But they didn't.

The soldiers took me through the building, asking whoever was at home if they knew of any relatives my family might have. They shook their heads with pitiful looks in their eyes.

"Okay, Joey, we're going back to the base," one of the soldiers said, placing a gentle hand on my shoulder.

"Can we go to heaven first?" I asked hopefully.

That's the line all the news broadcasts focused on. I know, because I've watched the tapes too many times to count.

A British politician and his wife made the first bid to adopt me. Once it got out that they'd offered the Croatian

3

government $100,000 for me, things started getting crazy. A Saudi prince, hoping to improve his image after one of his relatives blew up an embassy, doubled their offer and threw in one of his finest Arabian horses as a symbol of good intent. A French industrialist who'd made his fortune exploiting the people and resources of a small third-world country upped the price to $400,000 and promised another half million to care for other orphans of the war. There were bids from Japan, Canada, Australia, and Germany, but the Americans were not to be outdone when it came to generosity. At least four American couples made offers to adopt me.

Greta Powell and Robert Francis had been featured in tabloid headlines for months—ever since a paparazzo's long-distance lens had caught them together on what they thought was an isolated beach in Thailand. Their spouses weren't too happy about it, but Greta and Robert became bigger stars than ever.

Greta and Robert had just returned from their honeymoon in Cancún when they heard about the British politician's offer to adopt me. My soon-to-be parents set their publicity and legal teams in motion. After hundreds of phone calls to lawyers, ambassadors, ranking members of the U.S. Congress, the UN, and the Croatian government, plus an appearance on *Larry King Live*, I was placed in the custody of just-married Greta Powell and Robert Francis.

Here's the final deal:

$600,000 to the Croatian government,

$400,000 to orphanages throughout the former Republic of Yugoslavia,

$400,000 to UNICEF,

$800,000 in legal fees,

and a commitment to produce an *Orphans of War* telethon with no fewer than fifteen A-list celebrities participating, valued at $1 million.

Total payment for one Croatian orphan: $3.2 million.

This is my true story. How it came to be told began three years ago.

one

Robert's attorney, Lawrence Weinstein, was the one who came up with the idea for me to write this book. He suggested I tell my "incredible and inspiring" story to celebrate the tenth year of my adoption. Empire Books, a big New York publisher, agreed and put $75,000 into my trust fund. I was to get another $75,000 when I finished the book.

Robert mentioned the idea to me at dinner a few nights before I went with Uncle Larry, as he liked to be called, to New York. Robert was leaving the next day to join Greta in Kenya, where they were going to participate in a "famine awareness mobilization" event before going to Greece to shoot their latest movie, *Blood Luster III*.

"You've got all summer to write it, so school won't get in

the way, and you'll be earning your own money," Robert said while carving a medium-rare steak prepared by our cook, Octavia. "And there's going to be a writer from the *New York Times* working on the book with you, so all you really have to do is tell him your story—he'll do the rest."

A thought flashed through my mind. "Can I write it myself?" I asked.

My nine-year-old sister, Guava, looked up from the peas she had been arranging into neat little rows on her plate. "You can't write a book," she said.

"Why not?" I said.

She thought about it a minute, then shrugged. "Daddy, can I write a book, too?"

Robert ignored her question. "Why would you want to write it by yourself?" Robert asked suspiciously.

He must have been thinking that if I wrote it myself, it would turn into the sort of tell-all book kids of celebrities sometimes write, revealing all sorts of horrible things, like how their dads only spoke to them four-point-five times a month or their moms treated them as accessories instead of as children, both of which would be true in my case.

"It'll be more fun that way," I said, wearing the same poker face I'd seen him use when he'd appeared on *Gambling with the Stars*.

"You're thirteen years old. What do you know about writing a book? No, no, we'll get the guy from the *Times* to be your cowriter."

The phone rang. Perhaps it was fate, or maybe it was just coincidence, but the caller was John Handleman, the publisher of Empire Books.

"Yes, he's totally on board. Very excited when I told him," Robert said. "Only he has this crazy idea that he should write the book by himself." He let out a little chuckle.

There was a long pause, and then Robert began to do a lot of nodding and repeating "Yes, yes," over and over again. It made me think about what he always said when I didn't do what he wanted: *You're in big trouble, mister.*

"Your dad told me, and I think it's a terrific idea," John Handleman said. Larry and I sat on a sofa facing him in his large corner office in midtown Manhattan. "This will make a great story," he continued. "A thirteen-year-old refugee writing a book on his own. Fantastic!"

"I think we just sold another fifty thousand copies," declared Margo Reiss, the marketing director, from a chair on my right. "Oh, did your father tell you? We're going to donate one dollar from every book sold—after cost, of course—to the International Relief Fund for Children."

John Handleman stared at me across the coffee table, which was strewn with presents—mostly kids' books published by Empire, but also a baseball autographed by Derek Jeter and an iPod loaded with songs from the BLAM music club, which was owned by the same company that owned the book publisher. It seemed that Empire, like me, had been adopted by a rich parent.

"Of course, we can't *really* let you write the book by yourself," Handleman said with a little conspiratorial laugh. "So we've hired a ghostwriter to help you. But it will be your book, believe me. And of course, your name will be the only one on it."

John picked up the phone and hit a button. "Janine, is Tom Dolan here? Great, send him in."

"You're going to love Tom," Handleman said. "He's ghost-written several books for us. You know the autobiography for the band Watermelon Head? Tom wrote that. Those guys couldn't put a sentence together between the five of them."

"Six of them," chimed Margo.

"Right."

When Tom Dolan entered the room, he looked more like a baseball player than a writer. Sort of like Kevin Costner, except Tom was taller, had less hair, and wore glasses. I later learned from Margo that Tom had, in fact, played minor league baseball.

John explained how the process would work: Tom would come over to our house five mornings a week and I'd tell him my story. Simple as that.

It seemed to me that the ghostwriter setup wasn't all that different from the cowriter one, except that it would give the *appearance* that I'd written the book by myself. And it was saving Empire Books a lot of money.

Tom said, "You chew gum?"

I nodded.

"Good. Cause I chew a lot of gum when I write, and I'm not sure I'd be comfortable chewing in front of a nonchewer. You know what I mean?"

I instantly liked Tom. Not because of the gum remark, which I thought was kind of lame, but because the look on his face seemed to be saying, *I don't take this too seriously and neither should you.*

"I like gum," I said.

"Great." Tom grinned. "Then I'll take the job. If it's all right with you, of course."

"It's all right with me," I said.

Tom held out his arm and we shook hands.

"Excellent," said John Handleman. "I'll have Janine draw up the contracts."

two

Two weeks later, I was sitting in our breakfast room when our housekeeper, Rulia, ushered Tom in. Guava had already been chauffeured to the Warner Bros. studio lot in Burbank, where her new television show, *Flavors*, about a family who runs an ice cream parlor, was in the middle of its production schedule. Robert and Greta were still upstairs—it always took them at least an hour to get ready in the morning.

Tom was wearing shorts and a Hawaiian shirt.

"Hey, Joe, how ya doin'?"

"Fine," I said, squinting as I looked up at him. The lace curtains Greta had had made by the set designer of her latest movie to be released (a modernized version of *Little Women* called *My Crazy Sisters*) were doing little to keep the sun out of my eyes.

A pot of coffee was already on the table, and Rulia poured Tom a cup.

"The security guard at the gate was ready to break me in two until I gave him my name," Tom said.

"You dress like the paparazzi," I explained.

"You'd think paparazzi wouldn't actually drive up to the guard gate. I always picture those guys hanging out of trees or perched on cliffs overlooking beaches." Tom must not have been aware that a paparazzo perched on a cliff had outed Robert and Greta as a couple.

"We had the gardeners prune all the exterior trees," Greta said, entering the room with Robert. Tom stood up to shake their hands. Robert was dressed to "take a meeting" (jeans, white shirt, sports coat, and Italian loafers) and Greta for a day of "power shopping" (sundress, sandals, and light, not-too-sparkly jewelry). My adoptive parents always looked like the movie stars they were, no matter what they were wearing: Greta with her bright green eyes, slightly upturned nose, and charming smile, and Robert the handsome leading man, with a strong build, intense brown eyes, and thick, dark hair.

"We like the round table because it's more egalitarian," Robert said, pulling out a seat for Greta.

I glanced over to see Tom's reaction to Robert's moronic statement, but he kept looking attentively at Robert as if *egalitarian* were a word everyone used to describe their dining table.

"I had Octavia make eggs Florentine for you and Joe," Greta said. Rulia placed a half grapefruit in front of her, then gave Robert his eggs Florentine, minus the English muffin and Hollandaise sauce. It was basically eggs and spinach.

"So tell us a little about yourself, Tom," Greta said, sprinkling a minuscule amount of artificial sweetener over her grapefruit with a tiny silver teaspoon.

"Do you have any ketchup?" Tom asked.

I knew from experience that his asking for ketchup would instantly diminish Greta's opinion of Tom. Although Greta had been raised in a middle-class family in the Midwest, she sometimes acted as if the Duchess of Windsor had reared her.

"I think we may have some tucked away somewhere. Rulia, would you see if you can find some ketchup for Mr. Dolan?"

"Thanks," Tom said. "Well, there's not that much to tell, really. I played ball in the Reds organization for a few years, and when things didn't work out, I went back to school—"

"You don't need to recite your resume," Greta interrupted. "We're familiar with your credentials. Are you married?"

"No, but I've got a girlfriend that I've been with for about ten years. Jessica. She's a writer, too. Mostly magazine stuff."

"You don't believe in marriage?" Greta pried, with the innocent frankness that had made her America's favorite female star.

"It's not that," Tom responded, not at all disarmed. "Baseball players are pretty superstitious, so if something is working, they don't want to change it. I played with guys who wouldn't change their underwear for weeks if they were on a hitting streak."

"So you equate marriage with underwear?" Greta teased.

Tom let out a short laugh.

"What about children?" Greta asked, her green eyes peering into Tom's face.

"What about them?" Tom said, chewing on more than his eggs Florentine.

"Do you have any?" Greta continued, like the prosecuting attorney she had once played in a movie.

"No."

"Are you planning to have any?"

I knew that it was just about time for Robert to interrupt when he said, "Let's not turn this into a talk show, honey," slightly annoyed.

"What? We're just having a conversation," Greta snapped back.

"Let's talk about the book," Robert said, ignoring her. "What's your plan, Tom?"

Planning was very important to Robert.

"Well, I don't like to work from a plan, exactly," Tom said, spooning ketchup out of a small glass bowl Rulia had just set on the table.

From the look on Robert's face, Tom might just as well have told him that he was a serial killer.

"Well, then how do you work?" Robert asked.

"I don't know. I guess we'll just start hanging out and talking and see how things develop," Tom said. He then turned to me. "Does that sound good to you, Joe?"

"Yeah," I said. I liked Tom's nonplan . . . plan.

Obviously, this didn't sound good to Robert. In a slightly disparaging tone, he said, "However you work is fine with us.

Everyone has their own process. Although it sounds like your process is not to have a process. But that's fine. Whatever works. The main thing is we want this to be an inspirational story. We want people to be uplifted by Joe's journey."

Journey was studio talk for what the main character of a movie goes through to accomplish his goal.

"Joe's journey?" Tom asked, even though I was pretty sure he knew what Robert meant.

"Yes. Joe's journey of having lost his family and then finding a new family," Robert said seriously. "People love that kind of story. They need that kind of story."

If Tom had any reaction to what Robert told him, he didn't show it. He was much better at hiding what he was really thinking than either Greta or Robert. So was I.

Robert, having made his point, finished his breakfast, wished us "good writing," and took off.

Greta smiled at Tom. "Don't get worried by all his film-speak. The main thing is that the story be personal. In Joe's own words . . . as best as you can write them," she said in all seriousness.

Greta took a last bite of grapefruit. "I'm still hungry," she said in a cutesy baby voice. She then shouted toward the kitchen, "Rulia, are there any English muffins left?"

"What's your earliest memory?" Tom asked. We were sitting in the room above our garage, which Robert had converted from a guest room to an office where he could write a screenplay. He'd worked on the script for about two days before giving up on it.

Tom's large black tennis shoes were on the coffee table, facing me. He had a notepad in his lap, but I quickly learned that he seldom wrote anything on it.

I was drawing a blank.

"Tell me about your mother. Your real mother," Tom asked.

I closed my eyes and saw my mother sitting across from me on the floor of our apartment in Dubrovnik.

"She was really pretty."

"Okay."

"And she was tall."

"Everybody's parents are tall when they're three."

"She was taller than my dad. My real dad."

"Okay, she was tall."

"And she loved me a lot. She played with me all the time and made me laugh. So did my dad."

I recognized Greta's step on the staircase.

"She wasn't like Greta at all," I said harshly.

"Who wasn't like me at all?" Greta asked as she came through the open door. "And honey, you know you shouldn't call me Greta. We don't want Tom to get the wrong impression, do we?" She ruffled my hair—which I hated.

"I was talking about my real mom," I said, looking up at Greta, causing her to frown.

"It's my fault," Tom jumped in. "I thought it would be

17

easier for me to keep track of who Joe was talking about if he referred to you by your first name. Sorry."

"No, no, don't worry about it. We're a modern family. We don't cling to titles. The point is we all love each other. Isn't that right, Joe?"

"Just one big happy family," I said sarcastically.

Greta looked like she was about to reprimand me for this snappy remark but decided to let it go.

"I have to go out for a few hours, honey." She then looked at Tom. "Everything going all right so far?"

"We just started," I said sort of grumpily.

"I asked Tom," Greta said with a slight edge to her voice.

"We're doing great," Tom said.

"All right. If you need anything, just ask Rulia. Nice to meet you, Tom." She smiled.

"Likewise," Tom said.

Greta went down the stairs. We listened to her Porsche starting, the car rolling down the gravel driveway, and finally the electric gate opening and shutting.

"Let's get out of here," Tom said.

"What about the book?"

"We've got plenty of time. Come on."

There was a small park not far from my house. When we got there in Tom's blue PT Cruiser, Tom pulled a baseball and two gloves from the back of the car. We found a spot away from the moms and nannies with toddlers and several homeless guys and tossed the ball back and forth.

"You want to go to a ball game this weekend?" Tom asked. "I have an extra ticket to the Dodgers-Giants game on Saturday."

"Yes, but I'll have to check with Robert and Greta," I said eagerly.

"Do you always call them by their proper names?"

"Pretty much. 'We don't cling to titles,' " I said, imitating Greta, "unless we're making some sort of public appearance, like at a movie premiere or a charity event. Then they want me to be all 'Mom and Dad.' "

Every toss Tom made came directly to me, chest high, while my throws were all over the place; Tom, however, casually caught the ball as if I were making perfect throws, just like his.

"I don't know why she cares if I call her by her name in front of you," I said.

"We're writing a book—that's a public event. Did you ever call them Mom and Dad? I mean, on your own?"

I knew where Tom was going with this: had I *ever* thought of my famous adoptive parents as anything more than famous adoptive parents?

"No." I shook my head.

"How come?"

"I don't know. I guess the adoption never really took," I said, half joking.

Tom laughed. "You mean like a heart or kidney transplant?"

"Exactly," I said, pleased that Tom got what I meant.

One of the homeless men walked up to Tom and asked

for money. Tom pulled out his wallet and gave him a ten-dollar bill.

After the man had walked away, I asked, "Why did you give that guy so much money?"

"I waste ten dollars all the time. To that guy it's a big deal. He can get something to eat, or use it toward crashing someplace other than the park, or whatever he needs to do."

"Robert would say you're enabling him."

"Yeah, I'm enabling him to get a meal. Speaking of which, are you hungry?"

I was always hungry.

Pink's on La Brea was one of Tom's favorite hangouts. We got chili dogs, root beers, and a basket of fries large enough to feed a village in one of the third-world nations Robert and Greta were always running off to raise money for.

"Tell me about Guava," Tom said, taking a bite of his chili dog.

"Well, she was born about eight months after Robert and Greta adopted me," I said.

Tom took a pen out of his pocket and jotted this fact on one of the tiny, thin napkins the restaurant provided. "What else?" he asked.

"She's crazy," I said, rolling my eyes for emphasis.

"Doesn't surprise me. You name your kid Guava, you're asking for crazy."

I was liking Tom more and more.

"You wanna know why Greta named her Guava?"

"Of course."

"Okay. Well, when Greta and Robert were on their honeymoon in Cancún, they developed a fondness for guavas. Greta says she named her Guava because she's the fruit of her and Robert's love. Isn't that gross?"

"It's only gross if I think about it, which I'm not going to do," Tom said, chewing, a little bit of chili sliding onto his chin. "So how is Guava crazy?"

"Well, for one thing, she thinks she's a princess." I pointed at Tom's chin to make him aware of the chili there.

"That doesn't sound so weird," Tom said, wiping his face with a napkin. "A lot of little girls, and some women I've dated, think they're princesses."

"No, she *really* thinks she's a princess. At one of our weekly family dinner's she announced that she was the reincarnation of Princess Diana."

"That's hilarious," Tom said before taking a swig of root beer. "Wait a minute, weekly family dinners?"

"Yeah, Robert and Greta are so busy that they enter 'family night' in their appointment books like they're scheduling some event they have to attend. And now Guava is as busy as they are. She just finished her first movie, she's going to be in a TV sitcom, and she has a CD coming out around the same time as her movie and her TV show. Greta is really into everything Guava does. She even gave up a big movie role this summer to be with her."

"Does it bother you that Greta is so devoted to Guava?"

"Not really," I said honestly. "She's like an extension of Greta; it's like they're one person in two bodies. If Greta has to go out of town for a movie shoot, she always takes Guava along."

"You never go?"

"No. But I don't want to," I said.

"If Robert's also gone, who takes care of you?"

"Nobody. I mean, Rulia is always here, and when I was little it was my nanny, Hana, so there's always someone around."

"How does Guava treat you?" Tom asked.

For the first time that day, Tom's questions were making me uncomfortable. "You don't take very many notes," I said, taking the conversation off myself for a moment.

"I remember everything," Tom said. "Sometimes it's not such a great thing. If it's something really important—a date, a name, some fact or other—I jot it down. I like to be listening to you instead of writing."

"Why don't you just use a tape recorder?" I asked.

"I tried that for a while, but for one thing, it sometimes makes people uncomfortable, and for another, I never ended up listening to it. Like I said, I pretty much remember everything. It's faster for me to write down any important details or ask you again later. Otherwise, I end up fast-forwarding and rewinding the tape recorder for twenty minutes looking for one little bit of information. Anyway, about Guava."

"She used to think I was pretty cool, and not just because

I was the orphan kid from Croatia. We'd make up games and stuff. But after a while she got all superior, and now she hardly ever says anything to me at all."

"What about friends?"

"Sometimes," I said quietly.

"Sometimes? That's a funny answer."

"I don't have that many friends . . . at least not right now, you know, 'cause school is out," I said, embarrassed.

"You don't have a best friend?"

"No. Well, I did. Max Haycroft was my best friend when I was eleven. He just kind of got me, you know what I mean?"

"We all need people who get us." Tom slurped, dredging the bottom of his root beer with his straw. "What happened to him?"

"His family moved to Seattle, and since then it's been hard to find people who . . ."

"Get you."

"Yeah."

"Listen," Tom said, wiping his mouth and chin with a handful of napkins, "you're just going through a friend drought. It happens."

"Really?"

"Really. Things change. New friends come along." Tom held out a pack of gum. "Want a stick?"

"Yeah, thanks," I said. "So who's going to the baseball game with us?"

three

Tom had four tickets in the reserved section along the right-field line. His girlfriend, Jessica, and a buddy of his named Rusty took up the other two seats.

I'd been to Dodger Stadium before, always sitting near the Dodger dugout, or in the seats directly behind home plate, or in the Stadium Club. One time, I'd even thrown out the first pitch. As usual, it was my dad's attorney's idea. Who needed a publicist when you had Larry Weinstein on retainer? Robert had gotten a lot of bad press because he had helped raise money for a relief organization whose leader—a friend of Robert's from college—had been taking two dollars for every dollar that went to starving children in Turkey, after an earthquake had devastated the country. Robert hadn't done anything wrong except put his blind trust in a college friend, but he was still taking a beating in the press. Larry figured that by bringing me out for some public events, they could deflect the negative publicity over the scandal. I was the symbol of all the good work Robert and Greta had done.

I was only nine at the time, so they let me throw the ball to the catcher from about twenty feet away instead of from the pitcher's mound. I got to shake hands and have my picture taken with the Dodger catcher. That was cool. But then some wise-guy reporter asked me if I thought my dad was making money off orphans and starving children.

"I don't know," I said to the reporter.

Robert pressed his hand hard into my shoulder and whisked me away from the reporter.

"Why did you say you didn't know?" he said, his carefully tweezed and separated eyebrows coming together for a reunion.

"I don't know," I said again, afraid of Robert's anger.

"Is that the only thing you know how to say? 'I don't know, I don't know,' " Robert mocked. "We're going home."

"What about the game?" I cried.

"There isn't going to be a game for you—or anything else—until you start to appreciate what your mother and I have done for you. You'd still be in an orphanage in Croatia if it wasn't for us."

Later, Robert made a rare trip to my room to say he was sorry. He said he'd overreacted at the ballpark, but I had to learn to be very careful with everything I said, especially to reporters.

"Reporters are predators, Joe. Do you know what a predator is?" Robert asked.

"They're like lions and tigers," I said.

"That's right, that's right," Robert said. "They have an acute sense of smell. They can smell blood and they can smell fear," he continued, as if we were engaged in a vital lesson of survival. "Well, reporters are like lions and tigers. And their victims are celebrities like your mother and me and you and Guava. And when they smell our blood, they move in for the kill, just like a lion or tiger. Do you understand?"

I was thinking, *You've got to be joking,* but I just nodded and said I understood and would be more careful from then on.

"You don't really think I did anything wrong, do you?" Robert asked.

"No," I said.

Robert gave me a pat on the shoulder. "I guess we both need to be more careful in the future," he said.

With Tom, it was fun to be at a ball game and just be a fan. But I quickly realized that you don't need to be a celebrity to get unwanted attention.

Tom's friend Rusty hollered at every umpire's call he didn't agree with and yelled in frustration whenever the Dodgers made what he called a bonehead play.

Tom, for his part, carefully explained the inner workings of baseball strategy to me, telling me why a bonehead play was a bonehead play.

Jessica sat on my left; I think she wanted to be as far away from Rusty as possible.

"How do you know Rusty?" I asked Tom between innings, when Rusty had gone to the bathroom.

"We played in a band together when we were in college. He's been going through a rough time lately."

"What happened?"

Tom took a look over his shoulder, just in case Rusty had come back. "He lost his job and then his wife left him."

"I'm amazed Kim stuck with him this long. I'm amazed *you* stick with him," Jessica said.

"He's not so bad," Tom said.

"Not so bad? He blew almost twenty thousand dollars from Kim's parents on gambling. And he was fired because he was playing online poker at work."

"Where did you hear that?" Tom asked.

"Kim told me."

Tom looked back at me. "Anyway, he's going through a lot."

"So is Kim," Jessica said, not letting Rusty off the hook. "And it's been especially hard on Gary." Jessica looked from Tom to me. "Gary's their son. He's a couple of years younger than you, actually."

There was a loud curse from the aisle, just above where we were seated. It was Rusty. He seemed to have gotten himself into an argument with another fan.

"You bumped right into me, you stupid jerk! Look at my shirt!" Rusty pointed at his shirt, soaked and dripping with the four Cokes that, a moment before, had been in the cardboard tray he was carrying. "This shirt cost me a hundred bucks!" he screamed. "It's a Tommy Bahama, you idiot!"

The fan Rusty was arguing with was probably close to eighty. Two young guys who looked like they could play pro football came to the old man's defense.

"What's wrong with you, man?" one of the linebackers yelled at Rusty.

"He's an old man, man!" the other linebacker screamed.

"Mind your own business," Rusty hollered back at them.

Tom was getting out of his seat.

"Tom, stay out of it," Jessica pleaded.

"It'll be okay," Tom said, making his way up the aisle.

My heart was pumping really fast when Tom reached the scene.

"Why don't we all try calming down," he said, reasoning with all the participants.

"Stay out of this, for your own good," linebacker number one said to Tom.

"Don't talk to him like that. He's a buddy of mine, and worth the two of you put together," Rusty growled. "You're the ones who butted in here."

"We just wanted to take care of the old man," linebacker number two said, looking around for the person he was defending.

But the old man had disappeared.

"Well, I guess that's that," Tom said, trying to defuse the situation. "Why don't we all go back to enjoying the game?"

That was when one of the linebackers called Rusty a dirty @#%. Rusty threw what remained of the Cokes on the guy, who responded by grabbing Rusty by the throat and forcing him to the pavement while Tom and the other line-backer tried to separate the two.

After a trio of security guards had escorted us all to the parking lot, Rusty was apologetic to the point of weeping. He apologized to Tom and to Jessica and to me. He even wanted to go back into the park to find the old man and apologize to him.

"I ruined everything," Rusty wailed.

Jessica had a *yes, you did, you jerk* look on her face but remained silent.

"It'll be okay," Tom said. "It was a lousy game anyway."

The moment after he said it, an enormous roar erupted from the stadium. It seemed to last for a full minute.

"I'll catch the replay on *SportsCenter*," Tom deadpanned.

We'd missed the game's highlight, but it was Rusty's mini-brawl that *I'd* be replaying in my head for the rest of the evening.

four

The morning after Rusty had gotten us thrown out of Dodger Stadium, we were back in the writing room.

"How did it happen, exactly?" Tom asked.

"Don't you do any research?" I asked back, not really wanting to talk about the day I'd lost my mother and sister.

"Some," Tom said. "But I'd rather hear it from you." He said it in a way that made me feel like he really cared, not like he was some reporter just wanting a story that might lead to a big paycheck or even some sort of journalism prize.

I told Tom everything I could remember, as if it were happening right in front of me. He just let me talk, without comments or questions.

When I got to the part where the soldiers took me to my

neighborhood and found the apartment where my family lived, it became more difficult for me to speak without crying.

"That's when they got the names of my mother and sister and the army was able to confirm . . ." My voice trailed off as my throat became tight. I took a deep breath and slowly let it out. ". . . That they had been killed in the bombings," I finished.

"Who told you?" Tom asked.

"No one. I overheard them talking to each other."

"No one said anything to you?"

I shook my head. "Nothing except that my mother and sister were with my dad in a better place. I knew they were talking about heaven. I started crying because my family had gone on a trip and not taken me."

"Okay," Tom said softly.

We sat in silence for a few moments, Tom scratching a few notes on his pad. When he had finished, he said, "How much do you know about your real dad?"

I hesitated before saying, "Not that much."

"Didn't your family, I mean Robert and Greta, do anything to find people who might have known him—or your mother, for that matter?"

"They made some inquiries, but most of the people who contacted them were more interested in telling Robert and Greta their own life stories than in giving them, or me, any information. Everyone thinks their life should be a movie." I smiled. "A couple of the letters were sincere. A man who had worked with my dad before the war said my dad was the

31

smartest engineer at the company and that he was kind and always willing to listen to others when they were having problems. He said my dad was the best man he knew."

There was something I wanted to tell Tom about my real father, but I wasn't sure if I should yet. What if he didn't believe me? The matter was decided for me when I heard someone coming up the steps. There was a pattern to how she was ascending: two steps up, one step back, two steps up, one step back. Finally, Guava appeared in the doorway.

"I thought you were at rehearsal for your TV show," I said, unsure if I was upset or glad that Guava had interrupted us.

"I finished and the director said I was great," Guava said, doing a shuffling tap dance into the room. Upon getting a good look at Tom, she stopped dancing and walked straight to him, holding out her hand.

"I'm Guava," she said.

"Nice to finally meet you. I'm Tom. You've always been gone when I've been here."

"I know. I'm in a TV show. It's going to be on Sunday nights on FOX."

"I'll be sure to watch."

"Do you want to go bowling with us? My mom said I should ask you."

I had completely forgotten that we had an event to go to that night.

"It's bowling for the homeless," I explained.

"The homeless are bowling?" Tom asked.

"No, silly," Guava said. "We're bowling for them because they have no money to bowl themselves."

"It's a charity event for an organization that gets people off the street and back to work," I said.

"Sounds like a good thing," Tom said. "Sure, I'll come."

"It costs more than regular bowling," Guava said.

"Well, it's for charity. How much?"

"It's a hundred and fifty dollars," I said.

"No problem," said Tom.

I didn't think it would be, having seen Tom give ten dollars to the homeless man in the park. He was generous without asking a lot of questions, as opposed to Robert, who, although he had far more money than Tom, wanted to be sure that every penny he doled out to the poor was used wisely.

"Nice!" shouted Guava. "I'll tell Mommy." She then bolted for the door and went down the stairs the way she'd come up: two steps down, one step up, two steps down, one step up.

"Where were we?" Tom said after we finally heard Guava reach the bottom of the stairs and tear across the walkway toward the main house.

"We were talking about my real dad."

"Right. Is there anything else you found out from people who worked with him or were in the army with him? Anything about him at all?"

There was but I still wasn't ready to talk about it. Not just yet. "No," I said.

"Okay. Why don't we call it a day?"

"Sure," I said, a little disappointed that Tom hadn't pressed me to say more.

"So what kind of bowler are you?"

"The kind that misses the pins," I said.

Tom laughed. "Well, maybe I can help you hit some of them."

five

At breakfast several days after the bowling-for-the-homeless charity event (where, with Tom's help, I'd broken one hundred for the first time in my life), Greta announced that Tom should accompany us on our trip to Washington. The President was going to present Robert with a Medal of Freedom.

"It will make a great chapter in your book," Greta had said to me at breakfast, before Tom arrived at our house. "I'm not sure Tom is getting the right impression of us as a family."

I was pretty sure Tom was getting *exactly* the right impression: our family was one big photo op. Once upon a time, families lived off the crops they grew on their land. Later, people began to live off what they could produce with their hands and minds. Our family seemed to live off having our pictures taken. It was as if we were some strange species from another world that would die if people didn't see our images on TV or in the newspaper. Every time our names were read or our pictures were seen, our lives would be prolonged until the next crisis of "lack of exposure" threatened us.

Whatever impression Tom had been getting of us, I was ecstatic that Greta was planning on inviting him to come to Washington—which made what happened next all the more enjoyable to witness.

Guava didn't have to be at the studio until later in the day and was seated at the round "egalitarian" table opposite me, eating a wheat-free waffle topped with strawberries and a tablespoon of whipped cream.

"I want more whipped cream. Send it back," Guava said imperiously.

"Honey, we're not at a restaurant," Greta said. "You know we don't want you to look pudgy on your show." I didn't think that Greta was being mean; she was simply talking to Guava as one actress to another. Even I knew the camera added ten pounds.

"I'm not pudgy," Guava protested. "Fine, then I won't eat anything," she snapped, pushing her plate away.

Robert walked into the room, dressed for tennis. He played doubles on our private court with a few of his actor friends three days a week.

"What's going on?" Robert asked.

"Oh, she just wants more whipped cream on her waffle," Greta said.

"After you wrap the show, we'll let you have your normal ration of sweets," Robert said firmly.

"I'm quitting the show!" Guava screamed. "I hate you!"

Normally at this point, I would have excused myself from the room, but since Tom and I had started writing the book, I had been trying to observe my adoptive family more objectively, and this was definitely worth observing.

"You want more whipped cream," Robert said sternly. "Okay. Octavia, could you bring us some more whipped cream for Guava's waffle?"

"Robert, what are you doing?" a worried Greta asked.

"I'm going to give her what she wants," Robert said, not taking his eyes off Guava, who had her arms crossed over her chest and whose mouth was in the tightest pout I'd ever seen.

Octavia walked in with the can of whipped cream. Robert took it from her. "Thank you, Octavia." He then walked over and stood above Guava, who reached for the whipped cream. Robert pulled it away.

"Allow me," he said, in a sweet but menacing tone. It was a line from one of Robert's early movies, in which he played a psychotic serial killer. You knew that whoever he said "Allow me" to would be his next victim.

"Robert, don't do this," Greta protested.

Robert ignored Greta's warning and added an additional dollop of whipped cream to the tiny amount already on the waffle.

"More?"

At once suspicious and impatient, Guava said, "Yes. Give it to me."

Robert jerked his hand away. He added another dollop. "How's that?"

"Give it to me. I'll do it myself!" Guava shrieked.

"Perhaps we'll allow you a little more. Just this once," Robert said. He was smiling, but I knew from experience that he was about to teach one of his children a lesson.

Robert once again held the can of whipped cream over the waffle and pressed the nozzle, only this time he did not stop at a dollop, a tablespoon, or even a cup of whipped cream; he kept going until the entire contents of the can had been emptied onto Guava's waffle. The huge mountain of whipped cream caused the strawberries and waffle to vanish.

"Is that enough for you? I can have Octavia bring me another can if it isn't," Robert said obligingly.

Guava, who had inherited Greta's fair complexion, was turning a reddish purple. Her tiny nostrils were flared and her normally cheerful hazel eyes seemed to flash red as she took in and released great lungfuls of air. I braced myself for the explosion. But to my surprise, she picked up her spoon and calmly said, "This is perfect."

She then ate the entire mountain of whipped cream, along with the strawberries and waffle beneath it, while the rest of us stared at her in disbelief. When she finished, she said, "That was delicious. Thank you, Daddy. I'm going to get ready for rehearsal."

If Guava got sick from the whipped cream, and she probably did, nobody ever knew it. I had new respect for Guava.

★ ★ ★

Two weeks after the whipped cream incident, everything had returned to abnormal (as opposed to extraordinarily insane) and we were all in the first-class cabin of a plane headed for Washington, D.C.

Greta and Guava were seated together, looking through fashion magazines, while Robert sat next to his lawyer, Larry. They were going over the speech Robert would make when the President gave him his medal.

Tom and I were in the row opposite Greta and Guava.

"How come Robert gets a medal and not Greta?" Tom asked. "Isn't she into all the same causes he is?"

"Yes and no," I said. "These days she's less into feeding starving children and more into feeding Guava's acting and singing careers."

I thought it was pretty obvious that Robert wanted to go into politics. The whole Medal of Freedom ceremony was one step toward his ultimate goal to run for office. Part of my duties as a trophy kid was going to fund-raisers and rallies for political causes and candidates Robert supported. I actually thought Robert might make a good governor or senator. It was like Tom said: whatever his motivations, Robert helped a lot of people.

"You know, I've never been to Washington," Tom said. "But you've been there a lot, right?" It was early afternoon, and the flight attendant had just set down our trays. Tom had gone for the steak, while I had ordered chicken and mashed potatoes.

"Yeah," I said. "One time I even spoke before a Congressional subcommittee."

"Really? Tell me about it," Tom said, cutting into his steak.

Robert and I were greeted at Dulles Airport by flocks of reporters and photographers. I was six years old going on seven, and this seemed perfectly normal to me. After all, the first time I'd ever flown on an airplane was when Greta and Robert had brought me from Croatia to Los Angeles, so I figured every plane flight from anywhere to anywhere else had hundreds of people waiting for you on either end of the journey holding cameras, notebooks, and tape recorders.

We were taken directly from the airport to Capitol Hill and into the office of Senator Preston Morgan of Iowa. Morgan was chairman of a special committee that Robert and I were going to testify before. The committee had been formed to determine whether the government was putting its money to the best possible use when it came to relief efforts around the world.

"Great to see you, Robert," Morgan said when we entered his office. "And how are you doing, Joe?"

"Fine," I said, taking an immediate disliking to the man, who smelled like aftershave and shoe polish.

"I got you a present," Morgan said in his oily way, and handed me a toy pickup truck whose bed was filled with stalks of corn. There was writing on the truck's cab door.

"That says 'Buy Iowa Corn,'" he said, a broad smile on his face.

"Thank you," I replied, not liking him any better for passing a toy on to me that I suspected had been given to him by someone else.

"You can play with it over there while I talk to your dad," he said, pointing to a corner of the room.

I didn't like his telling me what to do. I stood there for a moment even though I wanted to escape his smell.

"Go ahead, Joe," Robert said.

I did as I was told but listened to their conversation as I rolled the truck back and forth along the wood floor. Even at six going on seven, I was amazed at how oblivious adults were to the fact that kids pay attention to everything.

"With your help, Bob, the future is going to be very bright for the party," Morgan said behind his desk.

I tried to figure out whose party we might be going to later that day.

"I'm here to help get funding for those relief organizations, that's all," Robert said.

"Said like a true politician," Morgan laughed. "Of course, you know that I can do a lot more for these organizations from the Oval Office." The senator winked.

"You just tell me where to be and when," Robert said smoothly.

"And your Hollywood friends?"

"I'll see what I can do."

"Good. I knew I could count on you," Morgan said, rising

from his chair. "And you know when the time comes, the party will be there for you, too."

Was a party coming to our hotel room that night? I wondered.

The two men shook hands.

"See you this afternoon," Morgan said.

Robert called to me, "Come on, Joe, let's go."

Later that afternoon we were in a large room, sitting at a table facing a row of senators. Behind us were reporters and spectators.

"Would you mind answering a question for me, Joe?" a senator with a thick Southern accent asked.

I looked at Robert, who had told me beforehand what I would be asked and how I should respond. He nodded to me that it was okay.

"No, sir," I said.

Robert had coached me to say "sir" to any of the senators who addressed me.

"Very polite, I like that," the senator said. "Those of us from the South put a lot of value in manners. It shows respect for yourself and others." The Southern senator leaned forward. "Joe, if you had one wish, what would it be?"

"To see my mom," I said. "I mean my other mom." I looked at Robert, who gave me a slight, approving nod.

"Of course," the senator said, taking off his glasses. "Joe, like you, I lost my parents at a young age. I was lucky and had an aunt and uncle who took care of me. You've been lucky, too, having new parents who love and care for you.

42

But not all children are as lucky as you and me. So if you had one more wish for other orphans, son, what would it be?"

"That they could be lucky, too, sir," I said, as rehearsed. A flurry of flashbulbs went off.

"Thank you, son," the Southern senator said, putting his glasses back on. "Thank you for your bravery and your good heart."

The "that they could be lucky, too" clip was on all the news programs that evening, and before long the Senate approved a 25 percent increase in spending to poverty-relief organizations around the world. But even though some good came out of my performance, looking back, I felt like a little of Senator Morgan's oil had dripped onto me.

After checking in to our hotel, Tom and I spent the day going to monuments and museums. Robert was meeting with some lobbyists, while Greta and Guava were having tea with the First Lady.

"What's your favorite place in D.C.?" Tom asked on our way to the Vietnam Veterans Memorial Wall.

"The Air and Space Museum. I like looking at the capsules and space suits from 1960s when we put men on the moon. The chief of NASA led Robert and me on a tour of the museum once. I think I was about five years old. NASA was having trouble getting money for the space program, and one of

Robert's senator friends from Texas wanted to make sure the agency got all the money they needed to explore Mars."

Tom was flabbergasted as I described the way Robert carefully prepped me before the tour.

"Okay, Joe, listen to me," Robert had said. "When we're in the room with the *Friendship Seven* capsule, the man from NASA is going to ask you a question. Are you listening to me?"

"Uh-huh," I responded. I was a very good listener.

"He's going to ask you what you think of all this. And you're going to say: 'I want to be an astronaut.' Okay, say it back to me."

"I really want to be an astronaut," I said.

"That's right," Robert said.

"No. I *really* want to be an astronaut." I really did.

"Great," Robert said, "and after you tell him you want to be an astronaut, he's going to ask you why."

"I know," I said. "And I'm going to say, 'Because I want to go to Mars.' "

"That's great, Joe," Robert said, giving me a proud pat on the head.

On the news that night, you could see me saying my line, followed by the NASA chief saying the lines he'd also rehearsed: "Maybe it takes a child from a country that was stripped of its dreams to remind all of us of the American dream of exploring space. Hopefully, Joe, with a little help from Congress, you can one day live your dream."

"You *are* living a lot of kids' dream life," Tom said after I'd finished the story. We were walking across the Mall to the Vietnam Veterans Memorial Wall.

I knew Tom was right, but that was the thing: like a dream, my life never seemed quite real. I often wondered if I'd have felt this way if I had been adopted at two instead of three; then I might not have had any memory of my real parents and sister, and if I didn't have those memories, maybe I would call Robert Dad and Greta Mom. Or what if my adoptive parents were not two of the biggest movie stars in the world? What would my life be like then?

"You're not so different," Tom said kindly, reading my thoughts. He pointed to the wall as we walked alongside it, looking at the names of those who had died in the war in Vietnam.

"Everyone here was someone's father or son or husband." He came to a stop, then reached out toward the wall and touched an engraved name: JOHN DOLAN.

"I was five when he died. He was a helicopter pilot," Tom said quietly.

There was a ton of questions I wanted to ask him: Do you remember him much? How did it happen? What was it like at home after you found out? But I didn't ask him anything. If there had been a wall in Dubrovnik for men and women who had died in the war in Croatia and I had been looking at the names of my mom, dad, and sister, I think I just would have wanted a moment alone with them.

Because the truth of the matter was, no matter how many opportunities I'd been given by living with Robert, Greta, and Guava, I always felt like an outsider with them; I didn't belong and I didn't want to belong. I wanted my real family back.

My trophy-kid duties were light that evening. It was Robert's night to be honored; I was just there to help project the image of a happy family.

Tom sat next to me at the awards dinner and seemed to enjoy the whole thing. Robert and Greta looked like royalty, and Guava looked bored beyond belief. Her restless, swinging legs constantly kicked me under the table. Other award recipients that night were a former basketball player, a chemist, a diplomat, a TV talk-show host, and an economist. But all I kept thinking about was that moment at the wall when Tom had reached out and touched the engraved name of his father.

Robert had an important meeting with a studio chief the next day, so we flew back to L.A. on the red-eye. I liked flying at night. It was quiet on the plane, and there was something about being in all that blackness so far off the ground that made me feel like anything was possible.

I was happy that Tom had taken the trip with us. There were so many things I wanted to tell him now that I was beginning to trust that he'd understand. But going to the Vietnam Memorial seemed to have taken a lot out of him, and he fell asleep almost immediately after the plane took off. Maybe that was for the best. If I'd told him what I really wanted to tell him, he might have thought I was crazy, or worse, he might have pitied me—and that would have ruined everything.

six

The Fourth of July was always a big deal at our house. Every year about 150 guests would show up for the Independence Day extravaganza. They were mostly Robert and Greta's friends and colleagues from the entertainment business, many of whom brought their children. The party was always catered by one of the best restaurants in Beverly Hills or Hollywood, and featured a popular rock band on a stage that had been set up in the backyard. My favorite part was the fireworks show they put on after it got dark. This year was special for me because Greta had invited Tom and Jessica. They were among the first to arrive, around six o'clock.

Tom and I tagged along as Greta gave Jessica a tour of the house. Jessica kept saying, "Tom, can you believe this?" as we went from room to room. "Why didn't you tell me how great their house is?"

"It's incredible," agreed Tom, but it was obvious that he wasn't all that interested in the curtains, rugs, and tile flooring that were sending Jessica into rapturous envy.

We came back downstairs and Greta opened the French doors to the library. Robert was sitting in his favorite chair. It was made of extremely expensive leather, a color Greta described as "Napa Valley Cabernet." The chair was always strategically placed in front of the built-in bookshelves that lined the walls of the library, instead of behind his large oak desk. If Robert was a meeting with a Hollywood producer, the chair was set in front of a collection of great literary works and art books that would make a librarian drool. However, if Robert was meeting with one of his political friends or someone seeking his backing for a charitable organization, the chair was placed in front of an assortment of significant books on history and philosophy, and biographies of great men and women.

That evening, Robert had positioned the chair in front of the nonfiction wall of books; obviously, this was a political meeting. Robert was dressed in tan linen slacks and a crisp, short-sleeved white shirt. The two men facing him both wore dark pants and sports coats, despite the fact that the temperature outside was around ninety degrees.

"Sorry," Greta said, acting surprised to see the room occupied. "I didn't think anyone was in here."

I was pretty sure she just wanted to see who Robert was in there with.

"That's all right," Robert said. "We'll be finished in a minute."

Greta closed the doors. "Those guys want Robert to run for Senate next year," she said, leading us away from the library and toward the sunroom.

She'd finally said something that seemed to pique Tom's interest.

"Do you think he'll run?" Tom asked.

"Yes, of course he will. He's wanted to run for office for years," Greta said with some bitterness.

"You don't want him to?" Jessica asked.

"It doesn't matter what I want," Greta said. "Isn't this a great room?" she chirped as we entered the sunroom. "Joe, you should practice your speech. Tom can help you while I find out from Jessica why he hasn't proposed to her."

Jessica gave Tom a *don't abandon me* look, but Tom just smiled and said, "Okay."

"Let's go up to the writing room," I said.

A few minutes later we were in the room above the garage.

"Why do you have to make a speech?" Tom asked incredulously. After having worked on the book with me for almost a month, he still could be jaw droppingly surprised by some of the things I had to do as a trophy kid.

"I have to make speeches. It's how I earn my room and board," I said dryly.

"Very funny. . . . How long has this been going on?" Tom asked with some trepidation.

"Pretty much ever since I could read."

"You're joking. So does that mean . . ."

"Everything's written for me. Or for my character in the movie that's Robert and Greta's life, is more like it. You know, the one whose story we're supposed to be writing."

"This is unbelievable. Keep going," Tom said, fascinated.

"Well, at first I said clever things kind of naturally, but Robert couldn't always count on that. I might say something that could make him and Greta look bad."

"Like at the baseball game?"

"Exactly," I said.

"Right. So about your speeches?"

"Robert or Larry give me lines to say, or if it's something they think is really important, they hire writers to write for me."

"I thought that was just for the time you testified before Congress," Tom said, still having trouble grasping what I was telling him: that my public persona was almost entirely scripted.

I shook my head. "Usually it's just a line or two, like when I was seven and we went to the premiere of this science-fiction movie set in the future when there was no water. If anyone asked, 'Joe, what did you think of the movie?' my line was 'It made me thirsty.' "

"Pretty funny line," Tom said.

"It should be. A friend of Robert's whose job it is to make unfunny comedies funny told me to say it."

"Yeah, I've heard of people like that. They're kind of like ghost screenwriters."

"One time, when I was older, I think around ten, I told Robert that I felt like a phony saying all those lines I supposedly thought up myself.

" 'Everything we give you to say is based on who you are,' Robert said to me. 'We just want to make sure you're being yourself when we go out in public.'

" 'How can I be myself if everything's written for me?' I asked him.

" 'Because it's your best self,' he said. 'Based on your personality. People love you, Joe. Don't you like that?' "

"That is so messed up on so many levels," Tom responded.

"They hired you, didn't they?" I said, shrugging.

Tom nodded. "They sure did."

A worried look was on Tom's face.

"What?" I asked.

"If Robert is expecting this book to be about the you the public sees . . ." Tom broke off.

"What?"

"Nothing," Tom said. "Come on, let's go downstairs."

"What about practicing my speech?"

"I'm sure you'll be fine."

The band had already played a full set when Robert and Greta took the stage and thanked everyone for coming to their party. Robert introduced me by saying, "Our son, Joe, wanted to say a few words to you all." He then looked at me; I was positioned at the side of the stage. "Joe, come on up here."

When I got onstage, I wanted to say, My *dad's a big phony. . . . So is my mom, and so am I.* But instead, I gave my short, prepared speech, about being grateful for America and Americans like my mom and dad, and closed with "Everyone should forget their diets for the rest of the day, because the food is really expensive."

That, of course, got a big laugh, and everyone applauded when I jumped off the stage.

"You're good," Tom said, laughing and shaking his head.

One of the highlights of the evening was supposed to be Guava singing "Yankee Doodle Dandy," complete with tap-dancing and sparklers. Her act would lead into the fireworks display. It was a highlight, that's for sure.

At dusk, the music to "Yankee Doodle Dandy" came through the expensive sound system. Guava came onstage dressed like Uncle Sam, except with short, sequined pants. The crowd applauded loudly. Guava had a mike on the lapel of her Uncle Sam coat and loudly sang out the words to the song, strutting from one side of the stage to the other.

When she went into her tap dance, she reached into her coat and pulled out little firecrackers. This must have been her own idea, because all the color drained from Robert's and Greta's faces as Guava lit the first firecracker, tossed it onto the stage, and tap-danced around it until it exploded.

The crowd went wild. She repeated this action four or five times; the audience was eating it up.

Guava then lit another firecracker and tossed it onto the stage as before, only to watch it bounce and land on one of the band's electric guitars, which was resting in its stand next to an amp. The guitar and amp must have still been turned on, for no sooner had the firecracker gone off than the guitar burst into flames. There was a loud crack from the power amp, which suddenly had smoke pouring out of it.

A few screams erupted from the crowd. Guava was frozen, and everyone else, me included, was either in the same petrified state or looking around for someone else to do something. Finally, Robert jumped onto the stage and grabbed Guava, while Tom pulled a fire extinguisher from the wall at the bottom of the writing-room stairway and quickly sprayed the amp and guitar.

Once Robert had gotten her out of harm's way, Guava, in tears, ran into the house, followed by Greta. Robert told everyone to go back to enjoying themselves and thanked Tom for his quick thinking. Everyone applauded Tom, who looked slightly embarrassed. I was relieved that Guava hadn't been hurt, but I wished I had been able to do something to help her instead of just sitting there. I wished I could be more like Tom.

After a brief interlude allowing everyone to settle back into having a good time, the *planned* fireworks display went on without any accidents or surprises.

I sat with Tom and Jessica during the show.

"How come you knew what to do?" I asked as fireworks of all colors and shapes were lit on the tennis court, which was a safe distance from people and houses.

"Comes from playing gigs in a lot of clubs," Tom said, checking out the array of colored lights exploding in the sky. "You never knew what might go wrong. I got in the habit of knowing where the fire extinguisher was in every joint we played in. I kind of do it automatically now."

"Remember that night Rusty set his pants on fire?" Jessica laughed.

"What happened?" I asked eagerly.

A huge firecracker went off with a loud bang. The white light from it was reflected in Tom's glasses. He had a smile on his face that might have come either from the latest explosion or from the memory he was about to share with us.

"Okay," Tom started, "we were onstage and Rusty lit a cigarette between songs and without thinking tossed the match on the ground. Except the match was still lit, and instead of landing on the ground, it landed in the cuff of his pants. We were about a third of the way into the next song when I heard some strange notes coming out of Rusty's bass. I look over and Rusty's beating at his pant leg with his bass, trying to put out the fire. I found the extinguisher and sprayed his leg. It wasn't a big deal. The worst damage was from Rusty smashing his ankle with his bass guitar. He walked with a limp for about a month."

I was beginning to see one of the reasons Tom kept Rusty as a friend: a lot of great stories.

"This could have been a lot more serious," Tom said, referring to Guava's pyrotechnic display a short while before.

Robert came over and squatted in front of us.

"How's she doing?" Tom asked.

"She's still pretty upset. Greta's with her. Thanks again for putting out the fire. I owe you one."

"No problem," Tom said, as if putting out fires was just part of the job he'd been hired for.

Guava rejoined the party a little while later, no longer dressed as Uncle Sam but wearing a *Kids in the House* (her favorite TV show) T-shirt and jeans. I was surprised when she came over and sat by me. After a minute or two, she leaned her head on my shoulder. It stayed there until the last of the firecrackers did its business and dropped to the ground.

seven

The Fourth of July (and all its fireworks) fell on a Monday that year. On Tuesday Tom and I were back working in the writing room above the garage. Well, we weren't exactly working; we were playing Space Safari on Tom's laptop.

"Jessica and I are having a barbecue on Sunday," Tom said as he broke down the defense shield around my ship, which pretty much signaled the end of the game. "Nothing like you had here yesterday, but I thought maybe you'd like to come over."

"Okay," I said. I'd been wanting to see where Tom and Jessica lived but felt funny about asking if I could come over.

"Rusty's son, Gary, will be there."

"Oh," I said, going over to the sofa and then pulling two sticks of gum from the pack Tom had set on the coffee table.

"Jessica's niece, Martie, is coming over, too. She's about your age. But I thought it might be good for Gary to hang out with you. He's having a rough time with his folks breaking up, and Rusty—well, you saw him at the ball game."

"Why do you think hanging around me would be good for Gary?" I asked, sort of fishing for a compliment.

"You're cool," Tom said, without missing a beat.

Good compliment.

"Okay, let's see, where were we?" Tom said, pulling a legal pad from his black leather briefcase; the computer was only for video games.

I could hear Greta's familiar speedy ascent of the stairs.

"How's it going, boys?" she said with a smile upon entering.

"Great," I said firmly, trying to say *Can't you see we're busy* without actually saying it.

"Tom, how do *you* think it's going? Do you have anything I can read?" Greta asked, coyly.

"Not yet," Tom casually responded.

Greta, as usual, was undeterred. "Well, I'm not expecting it to be *War and Peace* at this point, but you've been working for a few weeks now, and it seems reasonable that you should have some pages I can look at."

"I don't like to show anything before it's ready," Tom said, standing, or in this case sitting, firm.

"Is that one of your superstitions?" Greta asked.

"You might say that," Tom replied, unfazed.

"Fine, then," she said. "Well, I have to return some things. Would you like Octavia to make you lunch?"

I looked at Tom, hoping he'd want to go out for lunch.

"No thanks," he said. "I think we'll go out." He turned to me. "What do you think?"

"Out," I said.

"All right, I'll be going." Greta focused her famously beautiful green eyes on Tom, and her normal cheerful smile disappeared. "I really would like to read something soon," she said, her words fired as precisely as the ammo we'd been firing in our video game.

Tom took a moment to respond. "Okay, you got it," he said. "I'll put together some pages for you."

"Thank you," Greta said, her America's Sweetheart smile returning.

"Oh, we're having a barbecue at our house on Sunday. Is it okay if Joe comes?"

"I don't have a problem with that, but I'll check with Robert. Bye now." Greta turned and sped down the stairs.

"Didn't she return stuff yesterday?" Tom asked.

"She's always buying and returning stuff," I said. "Dresses, shoes, tables, curtains, wine, pillows, rugs—"

"I think I get the idea," Tom interrupted.

"She would have returned me if she could," I said.

"You don't really think that, do you?"

"No. But sometimes I feel like I'm not the kid she thinks she bought."

Tom leaned forward, propping his right elbow on the desk and setting his chin in the palm of his hand.

"Who's the kid she thinks she bought?" Tom asked.

"The kid they take out in public. The one who's forever grateful to them and praises them for rescuing him from his pitiful, tragic, orphan life. I mean, what kid wouldn't want to be adopted by movie stars?"

"I know Greta and Robert aren't perfect, but they don't seem that horrible, either. In their own way, I think they're doing the best they can."

I was ready to tell Tom something important, something that would make him see how inept Greta and Robert were as my so-called parents.

"You don't know what it was like when I first got here," I said.

"Tell me."

Before I left Dubrovnik with Robert and Greta at the age of three, one of the soldiers at the military base squatted down and gave me a shoe box. Inside were photographs of my mother, father, and sister they'd taken from our apartment. There were also several small toys: a top, some hand-carved animals, a snow globe of Dubrovnik, and a tiny metal fire engine. Another soldier handed Robert a small travel bag containing some of my clothes.

I kept the shoe box in my lap all the way from Dubrovnik to Los Angeles; I even took it with me each time I went to the bathroom.

I held it tightly in the limo that took us from the airport to Robert and Greta's Bel-Air house.

When Robert carried me up the stairs to my new bedroom, I clutched my shoe box as I twisted and turned and cried to be put down.

While in Dubrovnik, Robert had hired a Croatian woman named Hana to be my live-in nanny and translator until I learned English. Greta had gone all out in putting together the perfect boy's room, and Hana explained that it was now mine.

The walls were powder blue. My little bed was covered with a comforter decorated with Winnie-the-Pooh characters. There were at least a half-dozen stuffed animals on the bed.

On the walls were framed cels from Disney movies like *The Little Mermaid*, *101 Dalmatians*, and *Lady and the Tramp*.

There was a Mickey Mouse dresser with Mickey stenciled onto the drawers, and a Donald Duck entertainment center.

There were tables on either side of my bed, one with the image of Aladdin and the other with the Genie.

I later found out that Disney had donated most of the furniture and even the highly valuable cels because the room was to be featured in *Home and Style* magazine.

There was a huge treasure chest that Greta opened, revealing dozens of toys.

"And look at this, Joey," Greta said enthusiastically through Hana.

Greta turned off the light: the entire ceiling glowed with stars. Even though I was amazed, I was determined not to like anything about my new home, so I kept my pout on.

After a moment, Greta flipped the light back on.

Robert finally set me down on the floor. "Do you like your room?" Hana translated for Robert.

I ignored the question, sat on the *Song of the South* rug in the middle of the room, and opened my shoe box. One by one I took out the photographs of my mother, father, and sister; the top; the hand-carved animals; the tourist-shop snow globe of Dubrovnik; and the tiny metal fire engine and placed them on the rug in front of me.

Greta tried to remove my old clothes and get me into my brand-new Goofy pajamas, but I refused to let her. She finally gave up and left the room, along with Robert, leaving Hana to get me changed, washed up, and into bed. Robert and Greta then came back into the room and attempted to kiss me goodnight, but I flopped onto my stomach and buried my head beneath my pillow.

When I awoke after my first night in the house in Bel-Air, the pictures of my mother, father, and sister, along with my old toys, had been placed on the Aladdin table on the right side of my bed. On the Genie table, there was a picture of Robert and Greta and me taken in Dubrovnik. In the photo, Greta and Robert wore movie-star smiles, while I had a surprised look on my face, like the photographer had made flowers appear in one hand while he snapped the picture with the other—which was exactly what he had done to distract me from crying.

I knocked the picture of me with Robert and Greta onto the floor. I then looked around for my shoe box. I wasn't planning on staying in this house and wanted to be ready when my real mother and father came back from heaven, or wherever they were, to take me home. It wasn't anywhere in the room, so I took the long journey down the stairs and screamed "box" in Croatian over and over again.

Greta came running down the stairs in her robe and found me trying to open the front door. I don't know why I was doing that. I guess I thought I might find the box that had transported my possessions outside. Or maybe I just wanted to go home. Greta pulled me away from the door and got down on the floor with me, trying to find out what was the matter.

"Box, box," I kept crying in Croatian.

By this time our cook, Octavia, had arrived on the scene, her hands caked in flour.

"Octavia, go get Hana. She's in the room next to Joe's," Greta ordered, in desperation. Octavia sprinted up the stairs, leaving a series of gradually fading flour handprints on the stair rail.

"Joey, what is it honey?" Greta asked, while holding me firmly in place so I wouldn't run off.

"Box, box!" I cried.

Finally, a groggy Hana, also in her robe, came down the stairs and asked me what was the matter.

"Box!" I said again.

"He is saying 'box,' " Hana said to Greta.

"Box?" Greta repeated several times, searching for meaning. "Oh, he must mean that old shoe box his things were in. Why would he want that?"

"Box!" I shouted louder than ever.

"Oh, my god!" Greta said, exasperated. "Octavia, look in the trash and see if you can find a shoe box."

Several minutes later Octavia returned with the shoe box, which now bore tomato stains, bits of egg yolk, and coffee grounds.

"Box," I said happily when she handed it to me.

I ran to the stairs and began climbing them. Hana picked me up and carried me to my room, with Greta following. Octavia had gone back to the kitchen to finish preparing breakfast.

Once in my room, I went to the Aladdin table and put all my possessions in the box.

"Oh, for heaven's sake," Greta said.

She then spotted the photo of her, Robert, and me on the floor. She walked over, picked it up, and put it back on the Genie table.

"Hana, please try to explain to him that this is his home now," Greta said. She then looked at the Goofy alarm clock that was next to their photo.

"Oh, no, I'm going to be late for the studio," she said.

Greta got down on the floor with me. I didn't look at her. "Joey, we want you to be happy here." She looked at Hana. "Translate," she ordered.

Hana translated, but I still didn't look up. Instead, I shook the Dubrovnik snow globe and watched the snow come down over my city.

"Joey, Mommy has to go to work, but when I get home, we'll make everything better for you." She cranked her neck toward Hana: "Translate."

Hana translated, but all I did was give the snow globe another shake.

"It's nothing, really, right? Do I need to be concerned? I should go to work, right?" Greta asked Hana, who, having only worked for Greta for a few days, was reticent to offer an answer.

"Okay, I'm going to work," Greta said to Hana, her voice uncertain. "Everything will be all right, right?"

"I will take care of him. Don't you worry, Ms. Powell," Hana said reassuringly.

"Okay. I'll call you in a little while. Bye, Joey," she said to me in a sweet voice, desperate to get even a nugget of sweetness in return. I shook the snow globe again, and she left the room.

My insistence on keeping my possessions from home in my shoe box continued into the next week. My face was in a constant pout and I screamed a lot.

Robert decided it might be a good idea to bring in an expert. A child psychiatrist, Filmore Moody, MD, PhD, and

SAG (Screen Actors Guild—Dr. Moody had his own show on cable), came to our house to assess the situation.

After spending forty-five minutes with me, during which he tried to engage me by playing games with blocks and with the stuffed animals that normally were huddled together on top of my bed, Dr. Moody told Robert and Greta that there were no easy solutions to the grief I was experiencing. It was imperative that he see me no fewer than two times a week until I "took root" in my new home.

Eight months later, despite all the games with toys, blocks, and stuffed animals; despite all the crayon drawings and the application of every known modern technique for dealing with my grief—including having me rip up countless photos of Robert and Greta (old head shots were provided by the boxload from their respective talent agencies) until I burned out my aggression toward them—I still hadn't taken root in my new home.

At that point Dr. Moody advised Robert and Greta that it might be best to let me adjust at my own pace and in my own way. He was leaving on a six-week promotional tour for his new book, *My Kid Would Never Do That: Ten Steps to Taking Children off Their Pedestals*, and would check on me at the conclusion of the tour.

Greta and Robert were not pleased. Why would they be? The entire world was in love with them, and this one three-year-old was ripping up their head shots with gleeful abandon.

Fortunately, an event took place that took Robert and

Greta's attention off me. Guava was born. They had their "love child," and the pressure was off me to accept them as my new mother and father.

Several weeks after Guava's birth, I took my belongings out of my shoe box and placed them on the Aladdin table next to my bed. On my own, I gave the battered shoe box with the egg, tomato, and coffee stains on it to Hana to throw away.

"You see how they are?" I asked Tom.

"What?" he said, looking up from his notepad, where he was probably scribbling a few key words for when he went home to write up the story. "Yeah, I guess so." It was not exactly the reaction I was hoping for.

"Tell me something lousy that happened to you," I said.

Tom let out a little laugh before saying, "All right, that seems fair." He thought for a moment. "Okay, I've got one. I was playing for Chattanooga in the Southern League. Double-A team for the Reds."

"What position did you play?" I asked.

"Third base. Anyway, I'd just gone four for four against the Carolina Mudcats, including a double and a home run. After I'd changed into my street clothes, the manager called me into his office.

" 'Close the door,' he said when I walked in. I was thinking I was getting a bump up to Triple-A and he didn't want the other players to hear. Ballplayers hate it when someone gets bumped up to the next level. It can be your best friend; it doesn't matter. That's one less spot on the roster for you.

"So Terry, that was my manager, says to me, 'Tom, I've got some bad news. Management has decided to cut you from the roster.'

"I couldn't believe it. I said, 'But I just went four for four.'

"Terry goes, 'Let me ask you something. What pitches did you hit?'

"I suddenly knew where this was going. 'Fastballs,' I said. 'They were all fastballs.'

" 'Exactly,' Terry says."

"Wait, I don't get it," I jumped in. "What's wrong with hitting fastballs?"

"Nothing," said Tom. "Except there's about a million guys who can hit fastballs. What gets you to the majors and what keeps you there is hitting the curve, and I couldn't hit a curve ball to save my life."

"So that was it?"

"Yeah. At least I can say I went four for four in my last game."

"Wow," I said. "That's so cold."

"That's professional sports. I still get the heebie-jeebies every time spring training rolls around."

"So is that when you started the band with Rusty?"

"No. I spent about six months doing absolutely nothing except feeling sorry for myself and thinking about what might have been. All I'd ever wanted was to be a profes-sional baseball player. Then I met Jessica, and she sort of made me realize that my life wasn't over. I'd been drafted by the Reds right out of high school and hadn't given much thought to getting an education, which my mom told me I'd regret. She was right, of course. So I enrolled in Pasadena City College and started taking writing classes."

"What about the band with Rusty?" I asked.

"I met Rusty in one of my classes. I think it was English lit," Tom said. "I'd been teaching myself how to play guitar; Rusty had been playing for a while. We started hanging out together and learning as many songs as we could. Pretty soon we were writing our own songs. Most of them were terrible." Tom shook his head and laughed. "I'm what you might call a professional failure."

"What do you mean?"

"Well, I've made money as a baseball player, a musician, and a writer, but I've never been good enough make it to the major leagues or get a record deal—"

"Or write a book with your name on the front cover," I said, finishing his thought.

"Exactly," Tom said. "But I'm not complaining. All in all, I have a pretty good life."

Tom's gaze shifted away for a moment, and then he looked me directly in the eye. "Robert and Greta may be movie stars and all that, but they're still just two people with an impossible task."

"What's that?" I asked.

"To raise a child who will never love them as much as he loves his real parents."

eight

"We've been getting into some things that I don't think Robert and Greta are going to be too crazy about," Tom said the next morning. "I mean, from everything you've told me, this isn't the book that is—how did Robert put it?—'based on your best self.'"

"I know. But it's about who I really am," I said. "And who they are, too," I added.

"That's the part I'm worried about." Tom sighed. "Okay, let's push forward. We'll put it all in and worry about the consequences later."

I smiled. "Good."

"Of course, I want to warn you, not worrying about the consequences has always gotten me into trouble in the past."

Tom pulled out his notepad. "All right, the last time we talked about your real family . . . I guess birth family would be more accurate, since your family here is real, too."

"That's a matter of opinion," I joked.

Tom just nodded. "You were telling me about your father. He worked as an engineer."

"A mechanical engineer," I corrected him.

"Right. Do you have any other memories of him that stand out?"

"Just doing what he used to call our gymnastics, which basically was him throwing me up in the air and catching me or pulling me through his legs from behind and then tossing me into the air. That was my favorite."

"And your sister . . ."

"Suzzie. She was a couple of years older than me. I mostly remember her teasing me until I cried. Then she'd tickle me, and I'd be so mad at her I didn't want to laugh, but I couldn't help it."

"Do you remember anyone else from your family? They didn't find any other relatives, right?"

"Not at the time," I said cautiously.

"What do you mean?"

I hesitated before saying anything else. I trusted Tom, but I still wasn't completely sure I should tell him this story.

"Something happened to make you think otherwise?" Tom asked.

I nodded but still didn't speak.

"What? What happened?"

★ ★ ★

It was my eleventh birthday. Greta threw a big party for me at the house, populated by children I didn't know and their celebrity parents.

I'd been looking around for Guava, who I'd overheard earlier promising Greta she wouldn't "steal focus" at my birthday party. That was when I noticed a bullish-looking man with a bushy gray and black mustache and pasty white skin standing in the corner of our sunken living room. He stood behind the grand piano, sipping from a plastic cup and stuffing mini-quiches into his mouth.

It was obvious that he didn't fit in with the actors, agents, publicists, attorneys, and other entertainment-industry personas who had brought their children and expensive presents to, for the most part, make a good impression on Robert and Greta, and to a lesser extent, celebrate the anniversary of my birth.

The strange man was searching the room, flakes of mini-quiche crust making a home in his mustache and on his white shirt, when our gazes met. He quietly set his plate and cup down on the otherwise-bare $25,000 piano and walked toward me.

"Josef," he said with wide a smile, revealing crooked yellow teeth, "I am your uncle Vladimir Petrovic."

Before I could even begin to process what he was saying or what it meant, he'd wrapped his torpedo arms around me and tears were dripping down his face onto my forehead.

"My brother, God rest his soul, was married to your father's sister, God rest her soul," he said with a heavy Eastern European accent. "We are relatives!"

I knew that what this man was saying didn't add up to his being a "relative." But in the "it's all relative" sense, this was the first person I'd ever met who had any connection to my real family, and despite the fact that he was pretty gross, I felt a little leap in my heart.

He pulled away enough to "get a good look" at me with his twinkly gray eyes. I was still in a state of disbelief when two of my father's security men swooped in, separating me from Vladimir Petrovic.

Security man number one said to Vladimir, "Please come with me, sir."

"But this is Josef," Vladimir said, pointing at me.

"We know who he is," said security man number two. "And we know who you are, and you've been warned not to come within two hundred yards of this property. Now please leave quietly with us or we will have to turn you over to the police. You don't want that, do you, sir?"

Before I could hear Vladimir's answer, security man number one was whisking me away, saying, "Don't give that man any concern, young man; we won't let him harm you."

I looked over my shoulder and saw Vladimir Petrovic looking over *his* shoulder as he was escorted toward the back entrance. I hadn't thought for a moment that Vladimir Petrovic wanted to harm me.

Later that night, after all the guests had left, I was in my room alone, halfheartedly unwrapping my gifts, when I heard Robert's voice over the intercom asking me to come down to the library.

"Close the door and sit down, Joe," said Robert when I entered the room. I sat in an overstuffed armchair opposite him.

"I'm sure you've been wondering about the man who snuck into your party this afternoon," Robert said in his most serious voice.

"He said he was a relative," I said anxiously. "Is he?"

"You're too young to understand this," Robert said, "but there are people in the world whose only aim is to take advantage of those who have more than they do."

I understood what he meant, but I didn't think it applied to the man who'd been whisked away by his security team.

"These people," Robert continued, "are too lazy or lack the skill to achieve success on their own, so they prey on those who *do* have wealth or talent, or in your mother's and my case, both. The man you met today is one of those people."

What was he saying? That the man who had identified himself as my "relative," Vladimir Petrovic, was trying to get money out of him? If that was his only aim, he was a better actor than Robert, because those tears rolling off his stubbly chin seemed real.

"This man," Robert went on, "started sending you letters several months ago."

"What letters?" I wanted to know.

"It's not important."

Someone who knew my family was sending me letters, and it wasn't important?!

"But I didn't get them," I said, totally confused and frustrated.

"No, of course not. Joe, I'm your father and it's my job to protect you . . . mine and my security team's. They check the mail every day for any suspicious packages. This man . . ."

"Mr. Petrovic?"

"Don't say his name," Robert said disapprovingly. "This man sent you several letters trying to establish a relationship with you. He's not a relative, Joe."

"I know that, but he said his brother was married to my father's sister. That's almost related, isn't it?"

"No, it isn't. All this man wants is money. He somehow got the name of my attorney—"

"Uncle Larry?"

"Yes, Uncle Larry."

"Uncle Larry's not really my uncle, but you let me see him. Why can't I see Mr. Petrovic? He's closer to being a real relative than Uncle Larry."

"You're confusing the issue, son. Don't be obtuse."

Yes, my so-called father called his eleven-year-old son obtuse. (I looked it up immediately after that conversation was finished; it means thick-headed or dim-witted.)

"When we refer to Larry Weinstein as Uncle Larry," Robert continued, "the word *uncle* is being used as a term of affection. Anyway, Uncle Larry and I met with this man, and—well, you saw him, he's disgusting. He said he was in the country for a short while and wanted to spend some time with you."

"That sounds okay, right?"

"No, not in this case. He wanted us to give him money to visit with you."

"Maybe he's poor and just wanted a little money to take me somewhere, like to the zoo."

"The zoo?" Robert scoffed. "When we told him we'd give him money *not* to visit you, he took it."

"Maybe he was confused," I pleaded in Vladimir's defense. "I don't think he understands English very well."

Nothing I was saying was having the slightest impact on Robert, who leaned forward in his chair and stared into my eyes. It reminded me of his performance in a movie when he played a hard-boiled detective who had to tell a woman she was never going to see her husband again.

"The only reason he showed up today was to get more money out of us. *Not* to visit you. I'm sorry you had to know about this, Joe, but believe me—all that man wants is money. I wasn't going to tell you this, but he has a criminal record."

"He does?"

"Uncle Larry did a security check on him. He was in jail in Croatia."

"What did he do?"

"He was a thief and he still is. Don't worry; we'll do everything we can to keep him away from you. If he makes another attempt to see you, we'll have him arrested."

"Maybe I have other relatives in Croatia he knows about," I said.

"You see the damage he's already done, filling you with false hope?"

"Maybe it isn't false hope. Maybe it's true hope."

"Are you trying to be funny?"

"No," I said. "He seemed nice."

"People like that always do," Robert said.

As was his usual practice, Tom had listened to my entire story without taking more than a note or two.

"Did you ever hear from or about Vladimir again?" he asked.

I shook my head.

"Do you think Robert was right? That all he was after was money?"

"No," I said, the bitterness starting to leak out as I spoke. "I think Vladimir just didn't understand English very well and was confused."

"What about his being in jail?"

"Maybe it was because of the war," I said. "Maybe he stole something to take care of his family. I think Robert totally overreacted and kept me from seeing someone who knew my family."

Before Tom had a chance to respond, I heard somebody bounding up the stairs. It was Robert in his tennis outfit.

"We need a fourth for doubles," Robert said to Tom. "You interested?"

"What about Joe?" Tom asked.

"It's only for an hour. You can get back to the book after we play."

"No," Tom said, "I meant what about Joe for your game?"

"That's not a good idea," Robert and I said simultaneously. The first and last time I tried to play tennis with Robert, he'd decided it was better to come over to my side of the net and correct my grip every three minutes, rather than have fun batting the ball around the court. Still, I appreciated the way Tom was trying to look out for me.

"We probably should keep going here," Tom said, also for my benefit.

Robert didn't seem to catch it. "Come on down. I insist," he said. "There's some extra shorts and T-shirts in that closet behind you. I'll see you in a couple of minutes." Robert bounded back down the stairs two at a time.

It wasn't easy to say no to Robert.

"I guess I'm playing tennis," Tom said.

nine

Tom hadn't played much tennis, but he had been a professional athlete, and Robert must have figured Tom could help him win a doubles match against two of his actor friends, Mickey Carlson and Trip Calloway. Contrary to what his name and his portly frame might imply, Trip was agile, and seemed to have endless energy. He raced around the court, even taking shots that should have been Mickey's. Tom, on the other hand, was playing almost as badly as I used to.

I sat on the sidelines and watched as the game went from friendly to fiercely competitive.

In the first set, Mickey and Trip trounced Robert and Tom, six games to one. Tom's timing and footwork were off, and although Robert kept saying, "That's okay, we'll get this next point," I could tell he was thinking that he should have pawned Tom off on Mickey and partnered with Trip instead. However, by the end of the second set, Tom's game had come together, and his shots were landing just inside the lines instead of just outside them. After they won the second set on an ace by Tom, Robert looked completely charged-up, focused, and determined to win the deciding third set. They'd already been playing for over an hour when Mickey tossed up a tennis ball and whacked it to Tom's side of the court to begin the last set.

Unlike the previous two sets, every point was a furious battle by the four men. And unlike the previous two sets, when Tom had checked in with me every once in a while to see how I was doing, in the last set his mind was totally on the game.

There were long rounds of volleys, and slowly the score crept up to five games all.

Then something horrible happened: Robert hit a great shot to win a point and give Tom and him a six-five advantage—and Tom high-fived him! Could it be that, through a tennis match, Robert had made a pal of Tom?

Robert served the next ball to Trip, who stroked it directly to Tom's feet. Tom managed to lob it to the other side of the court, and Mickey smashed it back down the line where Robert was positioned.

Please let him miss it! No more high fives!

But Robert didn't miss it. He dove, extending his entire body as far as it could reach, getting his racket on the ball and sending it back over the net, then tumbling out of bounds. This left Tom all by himself to chase down the ball when Mickey countered Robert's shot with a long lob to the back of the court. Tom hit the ball while running away from the net and somehow knocked it right between Mickey and Trip. Their rackets met each other instead of the ball, which bounced fairly on the back line.

I wanted to get to Tom before Robert could high-five him.

"That was amazing!" I said to Tom, who was huffing and puffing in exhaustion. Robert, equally thrashed, came up to Tom and gave him the dreaded high five. "Great game," he panted.

As they continued to congratulate each other I decided it was time to tell Tom what I'd wanted to share since I'd seen him looking at his father's name on the Vietnam Veterans Memorial Wall.

The next morning, as soon as we'd settled into the writing room, I said it:

"I think there's a chance my father might be alive."

"What?" Tom said, taken off guard.

"I think my dad might be alive, and I think Robert has been hiding it from me."

"That's a curve," Tom said, leaning back in his chair.

"And you have trouble with curves," I said brashly. I guess I was still a little upset about the way Tom seemed to have bonded with Robert.

"Touché," Tom replied, leaning forward. "Okay, I get that

Robert might have overreacted to this Vladimir guy, but how does that add up to your dad being alive? I mean, I'm sorry, Joe, but how could that be?"

"Someone made a mistake," I said.

After Vladimir Petrovic crashed my eleventh birthday party, I became extremely curious about my family and whether I might have relatives in Croatia who were alive. Maybe that was what Vladimir had been trying to tell me before Robert's security team had escorted him from our house.

I figured if Vladimir's letters had been hidden from me, then perhaps there were other letters from real relatives that Robert wasn't allowing me to see.

One night, when Greta and Robert were out and Guava was in the movie room watching *The Parent Trap* for the thirtieth time with Greta's assistant, Megan, I snuck into the library and quietly closed the French doors behind me.

There were two large wood filing cabinets behind Robert's desk. The first one was sort of an "ownership" cabinet. It contained documents relating to our house and the other properties Robert and Greta owned in Idaho and New York. It also held all the vehicle information: cars, a boat, and so on.

The other filing cabinet contained a lot of personal documents. Robert kept reviews, good or bad, of every play and movie he'd ever starred in or directed. Greta only kept the good reviews of her acting performances. Additionally, there were hundreds of photographs filed away. Every production had its own file, filled with studio stills, hair and make-up Polaroids, and personal photos taken with other actors and crew who had worked on the movie. Greta's favorites, and there were many, adorned the walls of the house or were placed on the tops of dressers, mantels, and counters. Also in this filing cabinet was correspondence from family and friends, and a few fan letters that had touched Greta.

There were even files for Guava and me—that was why I had snuck into the library. The file on me was quite thick. It could have easily been divided into two or three separate folders. There were lots of pictures and cards, and all the legal papers related to my adoption. What I was looking for were the letters from Vladimir Petrovic—and anyone else who might have tried to contact me—that Robert and his security team had confiscated. I was hoping Greta had saved them, but they were not to be found. I didn't think Robert would throw them away—he might need them as evidence to get Vladimir arrested or something—so I figured they must be at Larry Weinstein's office. I was placing the folder back in the cabinet when I noticed a yellowed letter-sized envelope at the bottom of the drawer; it must have slipped between the folders.

When I saw that the writing on the envelope was in Croatian, my jaw dropped. When I realized that the letter was addressed to my mother, I was filled with a mixture of sadness and joy. I heard Guava saying something to Megan, who seemed to be heading for the kitchen. They were probably getting some sort of treat, which meant that Megan would soon be going upstairs to my room and asking me if I wanted any ice cream or cookies, too. I quickly closed the cabinet and quietly snuck out of the library with the envelope from Croatia in my hand. I made it back to my room unseen and immediately sat down on my bed, opened the envelope, and unfolded the paper inside. In the upper right-hand side of the letter was some sort of government seal. The letter was postmarked August 4, 1995, two days before I'd wandered into the street in Dubrovnik. The date, however, was the only thing I could understand, as the letter was in Croatian. *Pretty lame*, I thought. *I can't read my own language.*

There was one person who could translate for me: Hana, my former nanny.

I hadn't seen Hana since I was five or six, when she'd had a quarrel with Robert and moved out of our house, but she had continued to send me a birthday card every year.

The cards from my birthday party the week before were still piled on my desk, so I jumped off my bed, ran over, and started going through them.

I found Hana's card and looked at the corner of the envelope to find her last name . . . but it wasn't there! All it said was *Hana*.

Her address was scribbled so illegibly that all I could clearly make out was *Los Angeles*. The street name looked like *Cwpivge*, which I knew couldn't possibly be right. Even the numbers were hard to read. Maybe I'd have better luck with a birthday card from an earlier year.

There was a knock on my bedroom door.

"Joe, it's Megan."

"Come on in," I said.

"I can't," Megan said. "No hands."

I opened the door, and there was Megan holding a small plate of chocolate chip cookies in one hand and a glass of milk in the other. She was in her late twenties, with naturally red hair.

"What are you doing?" she asked, handing me the cookies and milk.

"Nothing. Looking at my birthday cards," I said honestly.

"Oh, that's nice. Do you want to watch the rest of the movie with us?"

"No," I said, "I've seen it."

"Me too, but your sister loves it. Okay, well, come on down if you feel like it."

Megan had a *poor Joe, he's such a lonely kid* look in her eyes, so I smiled and said, "Maybe I will later. Thanks for the snack."

I set the cookies and milk down and went back to the door. As soon as I heard the movie start again, I left my room and walked down the stairs as quietly as possible. When I reached the library, I waited for a loud part of the movie and then quickly opened the doors and, once more, went inside.

I made my way back to the filing cabinets, but every birthday-card envelope from Hana in my folder was the same—well, not exactly the same. The street name on one looked similar to *Cwpivge*, but on another, it seemed to be *Srpiug*, and on another, *Zvviue*. The only consistent letter seemed to be the *i* in the middle.

Frustrated, I closed the filing cabinet too hard, and moments later Megan opened the library doors. "Joe, what are you doing? You know you're not supposed to be in here," Megan said.

"I . . . wanted to look at my old birthday cards," I said, doing my best to cast a look of equal parts guilt and sadness.

"You should have asked me," Megan said sympathetically. "I would have gotten them for you."

"I didn't want to bother you," I lied.

Megan came and sat with me and started pawing through the filing cabinet.

"I can't believe the way your mom saves everything," she said, shaking her head, "but it comes in handy sometimes, huh?"

"Yes," I said, "she even saved all my birthday cards from Hana."

"Hana," Megan said with a puzzled look on her face. "That name sounds familiar."

"She was my nanny."

"Oh, is that who she is," Megan said. "I just sent her a thank-you card for your mom."

WHAT!

I was pretty sure that Megan couldn't have read Hana's handwritten address any better than I had, which meant that I needed to look in the address book on Greta's computer.

"Megan, where are you?" Guava's voice ricocheted through the house.

"I'll be there in a sec!" Megan shouted back. "Here you go," she said, handing me the thick folder I'd just examined.

"Thanks," I said, walking with Megan to the library doors.

"Why don't you come and join us in the other room? You can look at your cards in there."

I suddenly felt guilty for deceiving Megan into thinking I was looking at the cards because I was feeling sad. But I had to find out Hana's address without seeming obvious. Otherwise, Megan might say something to Greta and Robert, and then I'd be back in the library, only this time seated across from Robert, who'd be quizzing me on why I wanted to contact my old nanny.

"No thanks," I told Megan. "I'd rather go up to my room."

"You sure?"

I knew that Greta's laptop would be in her and Robert's bedroom and wanted to get up there as quickly as possible.

"Megan!" Guava's shout came curling into the room.

"Oh, my God, can I come with you?" Megan sighed, closing the library doors behind us.

"Megan!" Guava shouted again.

"Coming, darling," Megan said sweetly.

Once again, I climbed the stairs and went to my room, but this time only to grab a piece of paper and a pen. Fortunately, Greta and Robert's bedroom was on the far side of the house, away from the movie room.

Greta's laptop was on the bed. I opened it up, turned it on, and found my way to her address book. It took a while, but when I saw the name *Hana Malendenka*, I new I'd found my former nanny. I rapidly wrote down her address (the street she lived on turned out to be Waring) and, even better, her phone number. I turned off the computer and darted back into my room.

I picked up the phone, dialed the number I had written down, and took a deep breath as the phone began to ring.

On the sixth ring, there was a click, and an accented voice came on the line.

"Hello?" Hana said.

I was suddenly scared. What would Hana tell me was in that letter?

"Hello?" she said again.

I felt as if I might be unwittingly entering a dangerous place, like a dark cave. But there was something to be discovered, and I had to go on.

My voice quavering, I said, "Hana?"

"Who is this?"

"Joe. Joe Francis."

"Josef! How are you? Did you get my birthday card?" Hana said happily.

"I did," I said. "Thank you very much."

"You are welcome. How does it feel to be eleven?"

"Sort of like ten, only older," I said.

"That's the Josef I remember. Always funny, even as a little boy. But I am thinking there may be another reason you have called me, other than to say 'Thank you, Hana, for your card, and all the other cards you have sent me on my birthday that I never called to thank you for.' "

"I'm sorry," I said, feeling a little guilty.

"Don't be. I am only joking, like you."

"Hana, I found a letter today. It was addressed to my mother from around the time my family was . . ." My voice trailed off. "Do you know what I'm talking about?"

Now the pause was on the other end of the phone. "Yes, I know this letter," Hana finally said very seriously.

"Can you tell me what it says?"

"You should ask your parents about this letter," Hana said.

"But if they haven't told me about it before . . ."

"Maybe they won't want to talk about it *now*, you are thinking. Yes?" Hana said, finishing my thought.

"I don't think they want me to know anything about what happened to my family before they adopted me . . . or even now," I added.

There was another long pause.

"This letter came a few weeks after they'd brought you from Dubrovnik," Hana explained. "It was from the Croatian Ministry of Defense. I told your father many times that when you were old enough, he must tell you about it. But he said it would be cruel to give you false hope."

"What does it say?" I asked, needing to know.

"It says that the government was mistaken when they reported to your mother that your father had been killed."

"My father is alive?" I gasped.

"No, it does not mean that, I am sorry to say," Hana said.

"But you just said . . ."

"What the letter said was that the body of your father was not found. The letter said that he was missing in action."

"So he might still be alive?" I asked, still astonished by what Hana was telling me.

"No, Joe, that is not possible. He could not have lived when the bridge was bombed. And after all these years . . ."

"Maybe he's in a coma," I said, not taking in her words. "Maybe he has amnesia and doesn't know his name."

"No, Joe, I don't think so. And it is not good for you to think like that," Hana pleaded. "Maybe I should not have told you this. I am sorry."

"Did the letter say anything else?"

"No, Josef, nothing else."

"Thank you."

"Josef . . ."

"What?"

"Your father could not have survived."

"But you don't know for sure," I said. "Nobody does, right?"

"Not absolutely, no."

"Thanks, Hana. Bye."

"Goodbye, Josef," Hana said, her voice filled with sadness. "You call me again if you need me, yes?"

"Okay, thanks," I said, and hung up the phone.

I looked at the pictures of my parents and my sister that had been given to me by the Croatian soldier so long ago and that now sat on top of my desk. My father looked so young and happy; how could he not be alive?

ten

"Did you ever tell Robert or Greta?" Tom asked, when I'd finished recounting how I'd discovered the letter saying my father was missing in action.

I shook my head. "I don't think Robert wants me to find my dad or anyone else who might be related to me."

"That doesn't make sense, Joe."

"It *does* make sense. If I found my dad or some real family member, he wouldn't have his trophy kid to take to fundraisers and help him become a senator," I said bitterly.

Tom didn't look at all convinced. "I'm sure he was just trying to do the right thing, even if it was . . ."

"The wrong thing," I finished his sentence.

"That was two years ago, right?"

I nodded.

"Have you learned anything else about your real father since then?"

"I wrote a letter to the Croatian Ministry of Defense. It was almost three months before they got back to me."

"And?"

"They didn't have any other information. Nothing."

Tom had a sad, pitying look in his eyes, a look I'd come to despise when anyone cast it on me.

"Why hasn't Robert ever taken me back to Dubrovnik? It's because he doesn't want me to know or think about my real family."

"Have you tried to talk to him about it?"

"No. It wouldn't do any good."

"You should try," Tom said. "He might surprise you."

I scowled. "So now he's your best friend?"

"What are you talking about?"

"Nothing."

"Is this about tennis yesterday?"

I didn't say anything.

"It was just a game of tennis, Joe. What we're doing . . . the book . . . telling your story . . . I'm with you on this."

"Do you believe me about my real dad?"

"Of course I believe you. Is it possible that your father is still alive? It's highly unlikely. As far as I know, none of the MIAs from Vietnam turned out to be alive."

"But it *is* possible. Right?"

"I suppose so."

"Don't say anything to Robert or Greta," I pleaded.

"I really . . ."

"Please . . . not yet, anyway."

"Okay," Tom said quietly. "Okay."

When we got back to the house after going out for hamburgers, there was a surprise waiting for us in the writing room: Greta. She was sitting behind the desk, skimming the latest issue of *Town & Country* magazine.

"Pages, Tom, I need pages," Greta said upon our entrance. Tom and I stopped short.

"I know you want to see something," Tom said, "but everything we've put together so far is pretty rough. When I—"

"Tom, you can deal with me on this, or you can deal with Robert, and believe me, I'm a lot easier to deal with than he is."

Tom nodded. "I'll have something for you by the middle of next week," he said. "So far, I've mostly been listening to Joe's stories and sketching out how those stories will be shaped. But I totally get your desire to see what we've been up to. Just give me a couple more days to put a few chapters together, and hopefully you'll be pleased with what we've done."

"That was easy," Greta said, seeming to accept Tom's offer. "I hate playing the heavy." I knew she was telling the truth. Whenever Guava or I got into trouble, she'd leave it to Robert to discipline us. I wondered if Greta wasn't so complicated after all; maybe she just wanted to be liked and to get what she wanted.

After she left, Tom said he was surprised Robert hadn't been more in our face about what we were writing.

"I think he's getting ready to announce he's going to run for next year's Senate race," I said.

"Really? What do you think about that?"

"I think it's going to make everything harder. I think that's why he and Larry want me to write this book. It's all to make him look good."

Tom took this in without comment.

"What are you going to give Greta to read next week?" I asked.

"I'll give her what she wants. I'll write up a few chapters of your story, the way they'd want it written. But I gotta be honest with you, Joe—that might be the only thing they'll allow us to publish."

"But we'll keep writing the book like we have been, right?" I said.

"Of course," Tom replied, smiling, but he didn't sound very convincing.

eleven

Tom picked me up in the early afternoon that Sunday and we drove back to Jessica and his house in Sherman Oaks. The place was tiny compared to our home in Bel-Air. It was a like going from the *Titanic* to a dinghy. Of course, the *Titanic* sank, so bigger doesn't always mean better. The living room was small and lacked the designer touches of our house. Tom described the decor as "early mishmash."

Dog toys and chewable treats were scattered everywhere; they belonged to a pair of golden retrievers, who charged into the room, skidding slightly on a patch of hardwood floor between area rugs, and leapt on me, practically knocking me over. "Sid, Nancy, get down!" Jessica hollered at the dogs. "Sorry about that, Joe," she said, pulling them off me.

"They're impossible. Come on out back. If you need the bathroom, there's one through the living room, and there's another one just off the kitchen," she said as she led me to the back door, passing through rooms that could have fit into Greta's shoe closet.

The backyard, on the other hand, was almost as big as ours in Bel-Air. Well, not counting the swimming pool and the tennis court . . . or the koi pond and gazebo Greta had had installed. There were several fruit trees, one filled with unripe lemons and the others with overripe apricots. A gazillion apricots had already fallen from the trees and covered the ground beneath them.

There was a patio area with a large round table and chairs shaded by an umbrella. There were also several loungers scattered about. An old barbecue was set up in the corner of the patio closest to the kitchen door. Nearby were several coolers.

"There's drinks in the coolers," Jessica said. "Tom, you should light the coals. I'm going to make a salad. Make yourself at home, Joe."

After Tom got the fire going, Sid and Nancy came running over to us carrying slobbered-up tennis balls in their mouths. Tom and I kept throwing the balls, and Sid and Nancy kept returning them to us with an additional pint of slobber, until Rusty and his son, Gary, came through the side gate.

"Hey, Rust, Gary," Tom hollered as they walked toward us.

"Hey, Joe, how ya doin'?" Rusty said. "This is my son, Gary."

Gary had dark hair like his dad, but whereas Rusty had a wiry build, Gary was pudgy.

Rusty opened the cooler and pulled out a pair of Sprites. He handed one to Gary and opened the other.

"Guess what? I joined Gamblers Anonymous," Rusty announced.

Gary looked at his shoes, embarrassed.

"Good for you, man," Tom said.

"Thanks. And I'm getting back into construction. I'm starting a new job next week."

"That's great," Tom said supportively.

"Yeah, well, I've got to make some amends, you know what I mean?"

Gary was still looking at his shoes.

I knew Tom wanted me to bond with Gary. But I had no desire to hang out with him. It didn't really have anything to do with Gary personally. I just preferred to spend time with Tom and Jessica and play with the dogs.

More and more people arrived. There were lots of introductions to people whose names I'd never remember. They all wanted to know what it was like having Robert and Greta as my adoptive parents. I gave them the answers I'd been carefully rehearsed to say since I was a young trophy kid:

"They're the greatest."

"We're just like every other American family."

"They're busy, but they always make time for me and my sister."

"I'm the luckiest kid on the planet. Really."

"Do you always talk like that?" a girl said to me after some adults had cleared away. She looked like she might be around my age. She was pretty. I mean really pretty. She had large deep brown eyes and long golden blond hair. A goofy smile spread across my face as my brain froze up. Even if I could have thought of something to say, the giant boulder in my throat wouldn't have allowed the words to pass through.

"Are you all right?" she asked. "You're Joe, right?"

I nodded, unable to open my mouth.

"I'm Martina, but everyone calls me Martie. Jessica is my aunt. She's great. She says you're from Croatia."

"Yes," I said, amazed by my own power of speech.

"So, you didn't answer my question," Martie went on. "How come you say stuff like 'I'm the luckiest kid on the planet'?"

How embarrassing to see myself being aped by this beautiful girl. I looked away from her, which somehow caused my brain to reboot and the boulder in my throat to dissolve.

"I was brainwashed," I said.

"Really?"

"No, but yeah." I shrugged. "My parents—I mean, my adoptive parents—are always afraid I'm going to say something that will embarrass them, so they drill me on what to say if anyone asks me about what's going on in our lives."

"That's ridiculous," Martie said.

"I know, but it's a hard habit to break," I said, daring to take another look into Martie's eyes.

"I'm going to talk to Gary," she said. "You want to come?"

Suddenly, talking to Gary seemed like a great idea.

Gary was lying on a hammock stretched between two trees at the back of the yard.

"Hello," Martie said, causing Gary to jolt and fall out of the hammock.

Martie started laughing. "I'm sorry, I shouldn't laugh," she said, but was unable to control her giggles, which were contagious; I caught them next, and finally Gary was laughing like a madman, too.

Gary then went into a routine where he repeatedly tried to get into the hammock and would fall out. Each time, he'd get a little closer to lying down before turning it over. Who knew that the kid who was staring at his shoes looking like he wanted to disappear was a natural comedian?

I spent the rest of the afternoon hanging out with Martie and Gary. At one point, Martie came up with a game where each of us would imitate someone at the party and the other two had to guess who it was. Martie did a funny impression of Tom flipping burgers, and I did a pretty good one of Jessica giving a tour of the house, but Gary was the best; he'd look across the yard, pick someone, and then do all their mannerisms to a tee.

We all avoided imitating Rusty, although I was tempted to do him getting in the fight at the baseball game, just to impress Martie. Luckily, I stopped myself. I think she would have thought less of me for making Gary feel bad about his dad.

I was having a great time. I couldn't believe that only a few hours before, I'd been wishing I could just hang out with Tom, Jessica, and the dogs.

Gary and Rusty left with the first wave of departees because Rusty needed to get to a Gamblers Anonymous meeting. When they said goodbye, Gary had turned back into the kid who kept looking at his shoes.

As the party continued to wind down, Martie's mom came to pick her up.

She looked a lot like Jessica, only taller and about ten pounds heavier. She also had black hair with blond streaks; tons of jewelry dangling from her ears, wrists, and neck; heavily made-up lips and eyes; and a large tattoo on her right arm of what looked like a series of intertwining cords.

Martie introduced us and told her mom I was from Dubrovnik.

"It is a beautiful city. Everyone should go there," Martie's mom said, looking nostalgic. "Very old, very romantic."

This description didn't exactly match the city I remembered, but I was only three the last time I was there, and there was a civil war going on.

"You should see it again someday," Martie's mom added.

"I will," I said, not sure when that day would come.

Martie seemed puzzled. "Who did you go there with, Mom?" she asked.

"None of your business. It was before you were born," her mom said demurely.

Martie rolled her eyes. "My mom likes to be in love."

"What's wrong with love?" her mom replied, causing everyone to laugh, while I stared at my shoes, like Gary earlier.

"We should go there," Tom said to me after everyone else had left.

"Go where?" Jessica and I asked at the same time. Tom was washing the dishes, and Jessica was drying and putting everything away.

"Dubrovnik," Tom said, turning to me and dripping soapy, greasy water from the pot he was cleaning.

"Tom!" Jessica cried. "You're dripping all over the floor."

"Sorry." He turned back to the sink, craning his neck to talk to me. "I think it would be great if we went back to your home. You could see it again and . . . well, I really think it would be good if we can try to make contact with this Vladimir guy."

I was shocked. "He's in Dubrovnik?" I asked.

Tom stopped washing, picked up a towel to dry his hands, and rested his back against the sink.

"Yeah, Rusty tracked him down," Tom said, grinning. "Rusty can find anyone."

"How did he do it?" I asked, incredulous.

"He called Larry Weinstein's office. He told Larry he was a federal investigator looking for information on Vladimir."

"Wasn't Larry suspicious?"

"He didn't seem to be. Rusty can sound very official. When Larry asked what it was about, Rusty said, 'I'm sorry, sir, but due to the serious and delicate nature of this investigation, I'm not allowed to give out that information.' "

"So where is he?"

"Larry said that Vladimir returned to Croatia right after he tried to see you a couple of years ago. He said he got one more letter from Vladimir, but he didn't keep it. All he could remember was that it was written on some hotel's stationery."

"Maybe he works at a hotel," I said.

"Or maybe he didn't have a home to go to when he went back to Dubrovnik," Jessica suggested.

"Or maybe he was really poor and couldn't afford to get his own apartment. I've heard of really poor people living in motels," I said.

"Or maybe he's really rich and can afford to live in a hotel," Tom said.

Somehow I doubted the man who'd crashed my eleventh birthday party looking like he'd bought all his clothes at a Salvation Army thrift store could be rich. "At any rate," Tom said, "Rusty bought a copy of a recent Dubrovnik telephone directory over the Internet. He found dozens of Vladimir Petrovics. I guess it's sort of like being named Bill Thomas here. We can try to find him when we go there. And more importantly, we can try to find out what happened to your father. I've been thinking about it a lot, and you need to know, simple as that."

Jessica stopped what she was doing, a concerned look on her face as she spoke to Tom. "Do you think this is a good idea?" She then looked at me. "I know it's none of my business, Joe, but shouldn't you tell Robert and Greta that you know about your father? Tom told me. I hope that's all right."

"It's all right. I don't mind," I said. "But I can't tell them. I just can't. It would become all about them. And . . ."

"What?" Tom asked.

"I want to keep this for myself."

"I understand," Tom said. "Let's see if we can keep it quiet. I think they'll get behind the idea of you going back home. We can tell Robert it's all part of 'the journey' you're on," Tom said dramatically.

Jessica still looked wary. "I don't know, Tom. You're liable to make a whole lot of trouble for Joe and for yourself," she said.

"Yeah, maybe," Tom said. "What do you think, Joe?"

Tom and Jessica stared at me.

"When do we go?" I said, grinning.

twelve

"It's such a beautiful day, I thought we should have breakfast outside," Greta said as Tom and I stepped into the gazebo Monday morning.

Guava had already gone to the studio; her final episode of *Flavors* would be taping that night.

"It is," Tom said. "Thanks for meeting with me so early."

A couple of hummingbirds flew in and stuck their long beaks into a nearby feeder.

"I feed them a cup of water and one-quarter cup of sugar. That's the magic formula," Greta said proudly.

"Sugar, who knew?" Tom said.

Robert put down his newspaper. "I may need you for

doubles again this week," Robert said. "Mickey's in Hawaii on his honeymoon."

"See, Tom, getting married is easy. If Mickey Carlson can do it, so can you," Greta teased.

I groaned in unison with Robert.

"So, what did you want to talk to us about?" Robert said, getting down to business.

"Joe and I think it would be a good idea for him to go back to Dubrovnik."

"Good for the book?"

"Yes, and good for him personally."

Two more hummingbirds closed in on the feeder, joining their pals.

"That is really annoying," Robert said, referring to the birds hovering nearby.

"No, it isn't," said Greta. "It's pleasant having them around."

"One of these days I'm going to have Rulia move that thing."

Greta looked at Tom. "The only person on the planet who doesn't like hummingbirds."

A squirrel ran into the gazebo and grabbed a tiny piece of whole-wheat toast that was on the ground near Robert's chair.

"*This* is why I never want to have breakfast out here," Robert said to Greta, shooing the squirrel away with his foot.

"Don't kick the squirrel," Greta chastised him.

"I didn't kick him. I just moved him away. If you didn't feed them all the time, they wouldn't be so bold."

"You just hate nature," Greta said, knowing that she had gotten Robert's goat.

"I do not hate nature," Robert retorted defensively. "I just hate aggressive squirrels. Now, where were we?"

"Dubrovnik," Tom said.

"Right. Interesting. Just the two of you?"

"And Jessica," Tom said. "She thought she might do an article about the city now that it's become a tourist destination again."

"I see," Robert said, bouncing the idea around in his brain.

"What do you think, Joe?" Greta asked.

"I want to go," I said enthusiastically. "I really do."

Robert looked at his watch. "Let me think about this and talk it over with Larry."

Greta gave him a look as he rose to his feet.

"And of course with you, too, honey."

"Thank you very much," Greta said, her voice dripping with sarcasm. "It's nice to be included in these decisions that affect our family."

"Tom, help me out here," Robert pleaded.

"I really think Joe would get a lot out of this trip," Tom said, avoiding taking sides.

"Very diplomatic," Greta said. "Maybe you should be the one thinking about running for Senate." The edge in her voice revealed some bitterness.

"We'll all talk later," Robert told Greta pointedly before leaving the gazebo.

"Well, I don't know what we need to discuss," Greta said to us. "I think it's a great idea."

I wasn't sure if she really thought it was a great idea or

just wanted to show Robert up. Either way, it was good to have her on my side.

Then, in typical Greta fashion, she switched topics. "You and Jessica should come to the taping tonight," she said brightly to Tom. "It's Guava's last show, and I know she'd love it if you were there."

I was pretty sure that Guava didn't care if Tom and Jessica were at the taping or not, but I kept my mouth shut.

"I'll make sure Megan calls the studio and puts you two on the guest list."

There was no further discussion: Tom and Jessica were coming to the taping of Guava's TV show. I was happy they'd be there. And would be even happier if they could bring Martie.

"Well, we should get going, right, Joe?" Tom said.

"Not so fast. You still owe us some chapters, Tom," Greta said.

"I know. I'm still putting them together. You should have them—"

"This week, Tom," Greta said firmly.

"This week, that's exactly what I was going to say," Tom said with a smile.

The wrap party for *Flavors* was held at an Asian restaurant on Ventura Boulevard that had been rented out for the night. A long buffet table had been set up on one side of the room, and on the opposite side there was an ice cream bar with dozens of flavors. There weren't enough tables—there must have been about a hundred people—so mostly everyone stood around talking, holding paper plates filled with Chinese chicken salads and pork dumplings or bowls of their favorite ice cream.

Although Guava was just one of the ensemble cast, she seemed to be getting the most attention. Greta stayed by her side while cast, crew, agents, managers, and friends all came by to tell Guava how great she was.

I was standing with Tom and Jessica and, happily, Martie. Her mom had a date that night, and had been grateful when Tom had made arrangements for Martie to come with us. Jessica, after having worked all day and sitting through a four-hour taping, was begging Tom to take her home. Tom wanted to wait "just a little longer," perhaps to follow up with Robert about our proposal to go to Dubrovnik.

Sometimes people would come up to me and ask me what I thought of Guava's performance.

"I'm proud of her," I said, with trophy-kid sincerity. "She's worked really hard for this."

Tom, overhearing me once asked, "Did you mean that, or was it just for appearances?"

I had to think about it; the words had come out automatically. But truth be told, despite how obnoxious Guava could be, and despite the likelihood of her becoming even more difficult once she had a successful TV show, I *was* proud of her.

"I really am proud of her," I said.

"Did you tell her that?" Martie asked.

"Well, no, not yet."

"Come on," Martie said, leading me across the room.

We waited for some people to clear away. "Hey, Guava," I said, suddenly feeling awkward around my own sister. "You were great."

"Thank you," Guava said politely, as she had said to all the well-wishers who had come before me. Greta was standing next to her, talking to Guava's music manager, and Guava began tugging on her arm. "Mommy, can I have some more ice cream?"

"In a second, sweetie," Greta said without looking at her.

"Go on," Martie said to me.

"And I'm proud of you," I said to Guava.

Guava shifted her gaze from Greta, got out of her chair, and hugged me.

"Thanks, Joe," she said.

"You're welcome," I said.

I looked up. Greta was staring at me. "Wow," she said. "That was so sweet. You *are* growing up."

My face got warm with embarrassment. Why had she said that in front of Martie?

"Were you in the show, too?" Greta asked Martie.

"No," said Martie. "I'm Tom's . . . I mean, I'm . . ."

Now it was Martie's turn to be tongue-tied. Sometimes I forgot that Greta was one of the biggest movie stars in the world and could send people into fits of blathering.

"This is Martie," I said, coming to her aid. "She's Jessica's niece."

"Of course," Greta said. "Well, it's nice to meet you, and thank you very much for coming tonight."

"Sure. It was fun, and Guava, you were really, really great."

"Thanks," Guava said, sticking her chin in the air like Shirley Temple.

When we rejoined Jessica and Tom, Jessica was once again asking Tom if they could go home.

"Soon," Tom said. "Look, here comes Robert now."

"Hey, Tom, thanks for coming," Robert said jovially.

"Robert, this is Jessica's niece, Martie," Tom said.

"Nice to meet you," Robert said.

Martie got all jelly-legged. "I really liked you in *The Disappearance of Harold P. Stottlemeyer*," she said, fawning.

"Thank you," Robert said. "You know, that's one of my favorite films, too." He then gazed across the room. "She's something else, that kid," he said warmly. "Look at her working the crowd." I turned to see Guava doing a dance on one of the tables while one of Robert's security men spotted her in case she fell off.

I started to feel a little jealous of Guava for all the attention she was getting from Robert, but then reminded myself that he had kept information about my real father hidden from me. He'd gone through my mail and had Vladimir Petrovic, the only person I'd ever met who had a connection to my family, from seeing me.

"So, Tom, how do you think the book's going?" Robert asked. "Greta says you'll have something for us to look at in a few days."

"That's right," Tom said. "I just want to clean up the first few chapters and then I'll show you what we've got." I knew that by "clean up," Tom meant he'd be taking out anything Robert or Greta might find unflattering—hopefully there would be something left for them to read when he was through.

"I've been considering our conversation this morning, and I think it would be terrific if you went to Dubrovnik," Robert said, his eyes shifting from Tom to me and back. "It really makes sense for the book," he said to Tom.

What about for my life? I thought.

"When I told Larry, he had some good ideas," Robert continued. "I don't want to get into them here, but I think you're going to love what we've come up with. We'll set up a strategy meeting and go through all the details. This is going to be a great trip for all of us."

Across the room Guava was calling, "Daddy!"

"The daughter calls," Robert said. "Joe, come join us when you're ready."

As Robert walked away, Tom said, "Did he just say he's coming to Croatia with us?"

"I knew he'd find a way to ruin it," I said.

"What do you mean?" Martie asked. "He seems nice."

"What do you think, Jess?" Tom said.

Jessica fixed her tired eyes on Tom. "I think it's time to go home."

The Dubrovnik strategy meeting was held in the sunken living room of our house exactly a week later.

On Friday Tom had given Greta and Robert the promised first few chapters of the book; they were extremely impressed.

Tom and I had gotten a little more information out of Robert and Greta beforehand.

They had decided—probably with Larry Weinstein's help—that going to Croatia should be a family trip. I was disappointed but not surprised; everything with Robert and Greta was a production, and my returning to Dubrovnik was a *major* production waiting to happen.

Larry Weinstein and Megan were also at the meeting, along with a man Robert introduced as Cal Noonan. Megan was there to take notes, and Larry to consider any legal ramifications, as well as bureaucratic obstacles we might encounter with the Croatian government; I had no idea why Cal was there.

No meeting that Greta held would have been complete without tea and some sort of treat. For this occasion Octavia made a lemon cake. My favorite.

Once everyone had their tea and had gotten at least a few nibbles of cake, Robert said, "Before we get started, I have an announcement to make. I've decided to run for Senate in next year's election."

"Bravo," Larry said, though I was sure he already knew of Robert's decision. In fact, Robert proved it with his next statement: "Larry has agreed to run my campaign."

I looked over at Greta. She wasn't looking at Robert or

Larry; she focused instead on her piece of lemon cake, slowly cutting off a piece with her fork as if she were performing open-heart surgery (which she had once done when playing a doctor in the medical thriller *STAT*).

"Larry," Robert continued, "why don't you tell them how this all fits together with our trip to Dubrovnik?"

This was worse than I'd thought. Robert was using *my* trip to Croatia to launch *his* political campaign. I hated him more than ever.

"All righty," Larry began, looking at his yellow legal pad. "On August sixteenth, we leave for Dubrovnik, for Joe's visit to honor the events that led to his adoption by Bob and Greta."

The events? How about that my family was killed in a horrible, stupid war?

Greta continued to operate on her lemon cake, but Tom gave me the slightest of nods, which I interpreted to mean *Hang on, everything's going to be fine.*

"On the day we leave for Dubrovnik, Robert will hold a press conference announcing his intent to run for Senate. We'll be taking a private plane, and Cal and his crew will be along to document everything we do. Cal is a fantastic documentary filmmaker, and we're lucky to have him with us."

Lucky in this case meaning *We're paying him lots of money.*

I was fuming. Even before Larry Weinstein went further into the trip itinerary, I knew every moment would be planned out to maximize media exposure and promote Robert's image as a good-deed-doer in the eyes of millions of California voters.

For the next forty-five minutes Larry went through every detail of the trip. All I wanted was to be alone with Tom to figure out how we were going to deal with all this.

When Larry had finished, Robert said, "We shouldn't forget that this is an important trip for Joe, and we want to be sensitive to his needs. Some of this might be very emotional for him." Robert looked at me protectively and then turned to Cal. "So the camera crew needs to stay a respectful distance from him at all times."

"You got it," Cal affirmed to Robert, and then said to me, "We'll use long-range lenses to capture the moments without being intrusive. You won't even know we're there, Joe."

Yeah, right.

Robert concluded the meeting by thanking Tom for the "inspirational idea of having Joe return to his place of birth."

Place of birth? Obviously Robert didn't want to say my "home" because he wanted people to think that this mansion in Bel-Air with its sunken living room, pool and tennis court, and all the bedrooms, bathrooms, and closets was my real home.

"This is going to be a wonderful experience for Joe, and hopefully an enlightening one for all of us," Robert finished.

Greta got up, having uttered not a single word, and left the room, followed by Megan.

Robert hardly even acknowledged me at the end of the meeting, choosing instead to "talk about the next step" with Cal.

Tom and I went outside and sat in the gazebo.

"Everything's going to be fine," Tom said. "I kind of figured something like this would happen, didn't you? I'm just surprised he's tying it in to the Senate announcement."

"He always likes to tie things together. You know, the sum of the parts is greater than each of the parts themselves."

"Right, the credo of the modern publicist," Tom laughed.

"Or the modern egomaniac," I added.

"Greta didn't look too happy," Tom said.

"She doesn't want him running for Senate," I said.

"Yeah, I get it," Tom said thoughtfully. "The press can be pretty tough on politicians and their families. But listen, Joe, we're going to make the most of this trip, no matter what Robert and Larry have planned for you. And we're going to do everything we can to find out what happened to your dad."

"Okay," I said, wanting to believe Tom.

"You don't remember much Croatian, right?" Tom said.

"Hardly anything," I said.

"Then we're going to need someone to translate for us. Someone we can trust."

thirteen

"Hana? You want Hana to come on the trip?" Greta said, surprised. "That seems a little odd. You haven't seen her in how long?"

"I don't know, since I was five or six, but she sends me a birthday card every year, and I bet she'd like to come. I *know* she'd like to come."

"You do?" Robert asked.

Tom jumped in. "When Joe said he'd like Hana to come along, I suggested we call her first and see if she was available before coming to you."

"And is she?" Greta asked.

"She is," I said with zeal. We had called the night before. It had taken some convincing, because Hana would have to take time off from her regular job, but when I told her how important it was to me, she'd agreed.

We were sitting in the breakfast room, where hummingbirds and squirrels wouldn't disturb Robert.

"It would be cheaper to hire someone there," Greta said as she lightly buttered a piece of toast. She still seemed to be a reluctant participant in Robert's run for the Senate. About the trip, however, she was excited; not only for me, but also for Guava, who would get to see where I was born.

"I'm sure you don't remember this, Joe, but that woman was very difficult," Robert said as Octavia placed a bowl of whole-grain cereal, covered with every type of berry known to man, in front of him.

"I thought she was quite helpful," Greta said. She seemed to mean it, but she also might have been in one of her *I'm going to contradict everything Robert says* moods.

"She was very possessive of Joe, don't you remember?" Robert said to Greta.

Greta took a bite of toast. "I remember I was glad she was there, especially during that first year."

"Well, it always seemed like she thought she knew more than we did about raising him," Robert said sourly.

No kidding. The fish in the koi pond knew more about raising me than Robert or Greta.

Tom got the conversation back on track. "We just thought that since Hana knows Joe and was there when he was adopted, he would feel more comfortable visiting some of the places that might bring back painful memories if she was with us."

I felt a little uncomfortable with the words *painful memories*, but if they convinced Robert and Greta of Hana's importance to me, I could deal.

"That's very sensitive of you, Tom. Of course she should come along," Greta said, not seeking agreement from Robert. "And it won't cost us that much more. There's room on the Gulfstream, so we'll just have to pay for her hotel in Dubrovnik."

"She says she can stay with her brother," I piped up.

"Perfect," Greta said.

Robert seemed content to let the issue rest.

"I'll have Megan call her today to make arrangements." Greta took a sip of grapefruit juice and smiled. "I'm delighted that Jessica will be coming with us, too. Maybe the two of you can get some time alone, and you might finally make a proposal."

Tom's usually sure hands fumbled with the shaker he was using to salt his eggs.

"You're making Tom uncomfortable, Mom," I said, coming to Tom's aid.

"Well, someone's got to." Greta smirked. "Why not me? I talked to Jessica at the Fourth of July party and at Guava's taping, and she says she wants to get married."

Megan walked into the room. "I'm sorry to interrupt," she said to Greta, "but your agent's on the phone. She said it's important." She then looked at Robert. "And Larry wants you to call him at his office about some adjustments to the itinerary on the Dubrovnik trip." Megan smiled at me at the mention of Dubrovnik.

"Thank you, Megan," Greta said. "Tell Sandi I'll be right there."

Greta daintily dabbed the corners of her mouth with her napkin before standing up. "And Tom, I know a great jeweler who I use a lot. I can get you an amazing price on a ring."

"Thanks, Greta. . . . I'll think about it."

"Really?" Greta said, delighted.

"Really."

Greta left the room, obviously pleased with herself.

"Don't let her push you into something you're not ready to do," Robert said once she was gone. "She can be quite a force when she makes her mind up about something." He gave Tom a rueful smile and stood up. "I should get going, too. Tennis this afternoon?"

"Sure," Tom said.

"Great. See you then."

As soon as he left I said, "Sometimes he almost seems human."

Tom laughed.

"Are you really going to propose to Jessica, or did you just say that to make Greta happy?" I asked.

"Actually, I am thinking about it," Tom said, "but don't you dare say anything to Jessica, okay?"

"Got it."

★ ★ ★

"I don't understand," Jessica said while stirring the tomato sauce that was simmering in a pot on one of the stove's front burners. On another burner, spaghetti was boiling. Robert and Greta had said I could eat at their house that evening. The heat from the cooking food combined with the heat of the day was making me sweat. "If Robert and Greta are coming along, how are you going to find out about Joe's real dad without them knowing?"

"I haven't figured that out yet," Tom said, looking in the refrigerator. "Where's the salad dressing?"

"It's already on the table with the salad," Jessica replied. "Where is it you need to go?"

"Zagreb," I said enthusiastically. "That's where the Ministry of Defense is."

"Can't you just call?"

"Rusty tried—" Tom started to say.

"Rusty?" Jessica frowned.

"Yeah, I asked him to help out."

"Are you paying him?" Jessica asked.

"A little bit."

"Tom!"

"Well, that construction job got delayed for another week, and he actually found out a lot for me."

"Like what?" Jessica said, still not convinced that Rusty could do anything helpful.

"First off, even though the war's been over for a long time, there are lots of issues that are unresolved between the governments. There's Croatians living in Serbia and Serbs living in Croatia. The Croatians and the Serbs both want to make sure their citizens aren't persecuted for their beliefs or for retribution over what happened in the war. The same is true with the Bosnians and Serbs. Apparently, the governments have been reluctant to release information on MIAs. I guess they're using it as leverage."

"That's horrible," Jessica said, pouring the pasta and water through a colander. Steam escaped into the air, making the kitchen even hotter. "What else did Rusty find out?" she said, shaking the last strands of spaghetti out of the pot.

"Just that if we go to the Ministry of Defense in Zagreb, we might be able to get more information. Things they don't give out over the phone. Like what other soldiers served with Joe's father, who might be alive. Exactly where he was last stationed. And names of military hospitals that might have records of soldiers."

"We could go to those hospitals, right?" I said.

"Maybe," Tom said.

Jessica began dishing the spaghetti into bowls; Tom covered each portion with sauce.

"I know you don't want him involved, but couldn't Robert make this all easier for you?" Jessica said. "He's got friends in Washington. Can't they put some pressure on the Serbian government?"

"He'd make it all about his campaign, and there'd be all

these reporters asking me questions," I protested. "And if we don't find my father . . . it would just make everything worse," I finished.

Tom nodded. "Let's eat," he said.

We picked up our bowls and went outside to the patio, where we sat down around the table with the umbrella in the middle. It was still light out, and much cooler than inside the house. The dogs ran up to us, hoping to get in on the food action.

Ever since Tom had said we should go to Croatia, I'd been running a movie in my head. In the movie, I'm at a special hospital for people who have suffered physical and emotional traumas. The hospital is located somewhere in the hills near my home in Dubrovnik. A doctor leads me out of the main building and onto peaceful grounds filled with beautiful flowers and trees. Patients sit on benches or on the grass with family members or hospital staff. A man is sitting on a stone bench by a fountain, alone. The doctor leads me to him.

"There is one man here who we've never been able to identify," the doctor says to me.

We arrive at the bench by the fountain. The man looks up at me. He has blue eyes just like mine, only sadder and older.

"Joe?" Tom said to me.

"What?"

"I was asking you for the salad dressing. Where were you?"

I handed Tom the dressing. "Nowhere," I said, shaking my head.

"What about Greta?" Jessica asked.

"What about her?" I said, twirling some spaghetti onto my fork.

"Can you tell her that you know about your dad being MIA?"

"She'll just be upset that I never told her before. 'How could you not tell me?' " I said dramatically, imitating Greta.

That made Tom and Jessica laugh.

"She's not so bad," Tom said, pouring out salad dressing.

"I think she likes you, Tom," Jessica said.

"What do you mean?"

"I mean I think she has a little crush on you."

"You're crazy," Tom said.

All I could think of was Greta telling Tom he needed to propose to Jessica and Tom telling me he was thinking about it. As if reading my mind, Tom gave me a quick *don't say a word* glance.

The doorbell rang.

"Who could that be?" Jessica said, getting up from the table. A few minutes later, she returned to the patio. "It's Martie. Toni just dropped her off with a suitcase."

"What's going on?" Tom said.

"Who's Toni?" I asked. My stomach did a happy-nervous dance, knowing Martie was in the other room.

"My sister," said Jessica.

"What did Toni say?" Tom asked.

"She said it was an emergency and asked if Martie could stay with us tonight."

"What emergency?"

"A guy, of course. What else? She said she'd pick Martie up in the morning. What was I going to say? I'm going to help her settle in." Jessica went back into the house.

"What's wrong?" I asked Tom. He was squeezing his temples.

"Well, Martie's mom has some problems."

"What kind of problems?"

"Well, you know how Rusty is with gambling? How he can't help himself?"

"So he joined Gamblers Anonymous," I said.

"Exactly. Toni is kind of the same way except with bad boyfriends. She picks the worst guy she can find and then totally wraps her life around him until something goes wrong and they break up. It's just tough on Martie, you know?"

"What about Martie's dad?"

"He fit the mold. The last we heard, he was living in a trailer somewhere in the Northwest. He never writes or calls her."

"I guess in a way Martie's an orphan, too," I said. "It's lucky she has you guys."

"Hello, Joe," Martie said, coming onto the patio with

Jessica. Her voice sounded like nothing was wrong, but I could tell she'd been crying. Jessica brought Martie a bowl of spaghetti, and we told her about our plans to go Dubrovnik.

"Maybe you can come, too," I blurted out.

Tom and Jessica looked at each other.

To me it seemed like a great idea. Martie could get away from her mom, who might recover from the bad boyfriend by the time we got back.

Jessica said, "That's nice of you, Joe, but I really don't think that's possible. You have things to do, right, Martie?"

"Not really," Martie said. "My mom and I were going to go to Lake Tahoe for a couple of days, but I think that's off now." She looked a little embarrassed and disappointed.

Tom and Jessica looked at each other again.

"All right," Tom said. "Let's think about it. I'll have to talk it over with Robert and Greta, but maybe we can make it happen."

I hoped so.

fourteen

Having Martie join us on the trip was easy. Several nights later, we were all in the entertainment room after dinner, and Greta said to me, "Your friend is coming with us." Robert was watching the news while Greta and Guava were sitting on the floor going over the artwork and photos for Guava's upcoming CD. Having completed the first season of *Flavors*, Guava was now fully focused on preparing for the recording studio.

"What friend?" Guava asked.

"What's her name, Joe?" Greta said. "Something with an M, right?"

"Martie," I said, trying hard to keep the happiness out of my voice.

"I can't believe that mother of hers," Greta said, "abandoning her daughter so she can run off with some guy."

"Tom says Martie's mom has an addiction to bad boyfriends."

"Smart fellow, that Tom," Greta said, without looking up from Guava's photos.

"Do I have to share my room with the girl who's coming with us?" Guava asked.

"I told you, you and Megan are going to share a room."

"Great move hiring Tom," Robert said to Greta. "I sent John Handleman the sample chapters, and he was very happy with what he read. It's exactly what I was hoping for. Tom just gets it."

Wait until Robert, Greta, and John Handleman read what we'd *really* written.

"John says Tom has written some screenplays," Robert continued. "I might have him take a look at that script for the remake of *To Kill a Mockingbird* I want to direct," Robert continued.

"That's the first I've heard about it," Greta said, looking up from the CD artwork.

"I thought I told you," Robert said, keeping his focus on the TV.

"You're going to run for Senate *and* direct a movie?" Greta snapped.

"I'm also thinking of playing Atticus Finch."

"This is wrong on so many levels," Greta said, shaking

her head and throwing her arms in the air, as if appealing to some higher court.

Guava and I exchanged an *oh, boy, here it comes* look.

"First of all, *To Kill a Mockingbird* is one of the greatest films of all time, and it should never, *ever* be remade," Greta began. "Second, if you are going to ignore my advice and go into politics, I don't see how you are going to direct and star in both a major motion picture and a Senate campaign at the same time."

"Did you say *star* in a Senate campaign?" Robert interrupted. "This isn't a lark, Greta."

Greta ignored the interruption. "And third," she said, "if you think the public is going to vote for you because they think you *are* Atticus Finch, and not some ego-driven, megalomaniac actor from Red Hook, New York, then either you or they are stupider than I thought. . . . And you know, I have a lot of faith in the intelligence of the American public."

"Are you through?" Robert asked calmly.

"For now," Greta said.

"First of all, great films get remade all the time. It's a business, in case you hadn't noticed. A business that has been very good to our family."

Oh, brother, he's going to argue Greta point by point as if he's in a political debate. He's probably thinking this is good practice.

"Second," Robert continued, "I haven't ignored your advice, I simply don't agree with you as far as my entering the Senate race is concerned. The movie will shoot in the fall and leave me a full year for the campaign. And third, no one in Hollywood ever lost money by *overestimating* the intelligence of the American public. People want simple stories and simple messages, and if they see me playing one of the greatest moral heroes of the last century, they will get the message that morality is what Robert Francis is all about."

"Oh, my God, you've started referring to yourself in the third person. We're in deeper trouble than I thought," Greta said sarcastically.

"Daddy," Guava said, "if you become a senator, do we have to move to Washington? What about my TV show?"

"We'll still live here, honey, but we'll also have a home in Washington," Robert said.

"You'll see your father even less than you do now, sweetie," Greta said, stroking Guava's hair.

"What do you think about this, Joe?" Robert asked, surprising me by asking my opinion.

Judging by the politicians I'd met, I figured Robert would be as good as any of them, maybe better. But my main concern was the trip to Dubrovnik, so I didn't want to side with either him or Greta.

What would Tom say?

"I think you're both right," I said diplomatically. "It's a big decision that will affect our family and maybe even our country." I knew I was pouring it on a little too thick, but they seemed to be buying it. And I figured if you live with drama kings and queens, you sometimes have to use a bit of drama yourself.

"That's a very intelligent answer," Greta said, as if I had just totally agreed with her.

"Very much so," Robert said, implying that, in fact, I was agreeing with him.

"I just want to go to Dubrovnik," I said honestly.

Two weeks later and we were really going. The early-August heat was intense, so it felt good to be in the air-conditioned grand ballroom of the Hyatt near the L.A. airport.

Seeing Hana again was awkward at first. She was waiting near the front of the room when our entourage came in. She looked younger than I remembered. She was a large woman with wavy brown hair that went just past her shoulders. Her nose was long and pointed and her eyes were hazel. Upon seeing me, she rushed over and hugged me.

"Josef, look at you. You are so big!"

"Thanks, Hana," I said, a little embarrassed to be fawned on in front of Tom, Jessica, and especially Martie, who was ecstatic to be going with us.

"Joe, we need you," Megan called out from the platform that had been set up at the front of the room.

A short while later Robert was saying, "It is with the support of my family and those citizens who believe in making the American government accountable to the American people that I am announcing today my intention to become the next senator from the state of California."

It would be nice if he were as accountable to me as he prom-
ises to be to the American people, I thought, standing with
Greta and Guava at Robert's side.

A large ensemble of supporters, reporters, and cameramen
were present to witness Robert's announcement and take
photos of him with his America's Sweetheart wife, his
America's Newest Little Darling daughter, and his America's
Favorite Trophy Kid adopted son.

Tom, Jessica, Hana, and Martie were huddled together off
to the side of platform, next to Larry Weinstein, who, like a
ventriloquist, mouthed the words as Robert spoke them.

Robert effortlessly segued from his political campaign to
our trip to Dubrovnik. When he said, "In returning to Joe's
birthplace, the site of so much tragedy, we seek to find rec-
onciliation and newfound hope," Larry actually pumped his
fist and said "Yes!" like we'd won a sporting event.

Robert concluded by saying, "Thank you very much, and
God bless *all* of America."

I had to admit Robert was totally charming and looked
the part of the crusading public servant; if I'd been old
enough, I might have even voted for him.

When reporters asked me what I thought about Robert's
running for Senate, the words Larry had coached me on
came effortlessly: "He made my life better, and I'm sure he'll
do the same for everyone else in California."

But when asked what I was hoping to find when I returned
home, I said, "The truth." This was definitely not the answer
Robert or Larry wanted me to give. I wasn't sure why it popped

out; I was supposed to have said, "Peace." Larry said this would have the double meaning of finding Croatia at peace and finding the peace of closure from my own past horrors.

Once "the truth" had popped out of my mouth, I felt laser-beam glares from Robert and Larry, and was peppered with follow-up questions from reporters.

"What do you mean, 'the truth'?" one reporter asked.

"Has the Croatian government been hiding something from you, Joe?" asked another.

"Who's the lady? Does she have something do with this?" a third reporter asked, pointing to Hana.

My old trophy-kid instinct kicked in. "I want to make peace with the past is all I mean. Isn't peace what we all want?"

Robert looked relieved; Larry, impressed.

"And the woman you were pointing to," I went on, "is my former nanny and my translator for the trip." Hana looked uncomfortable with the attention she was getting, and Larry looked equally ill at ease with the focus on her. He quickly announced to the reporters that we needed to get to the airport, adding, "Thank you all very much for joining us on this historic day."

Our "Dubrovnik party," as we were later described on one newscast, made our way out of the hotel and into a pair of waiting limos. It was a short distance to the airport, where we were driven onto the tarmac. Our plane, a chartered Gulfstream V, was waiting for us, along with a throng of reporters and photographers. Security abounded; I guess Robert's simple announcement that he was running for Senate warranted all the extra men and women dressed in darks suits, wearing tiny walkie-talkie receivers in their ears and serious crowd-scanning looks on their faces.

After passing through the gauntlet of cameramen on the ground, we climbed the moveable stairway and boarded the plane.

The plane seated fifteen, which was exactly the number of people in the Dubrovnik party. It looked more like someone's living room than the cabin of an airplane, with a sofa, tables, and leather chairs.

Our security team—Rodney and Butch (neither of whom had worked for Robert when Vladimir crashed my eleventh birthday party)—was seated closest to the pilot's cabin. Next came Greta, Guava, and Megan. In the middle sat Robert, Larry, and Cal with his cameraman and sound person. I was seated in the back of the plane with Tom, Jessica, Hana, and Martie.

Tom draped the green corduroy jacket he had brought over the back of his seat. In his blue jeans and plaid shirt, he looked like he might be going out to see a movie or to the Hollywood Bowl on a summer evening and not traveling over seven thousand miles to a small city on the coast of the Adriatic Sea.

Jessica was helping Hana, who seemed a little overwhelmed by everything, to get comfortable.

I was still wearing the dress shirt and slacks I'd worn to the press conference. Martie, in a pink T-shirt and jeans, was across from me. "The flight attendant told me they have all sorts of games," she said. "We could play Scrabble or Monopoly or . . ." The list went on, but I was too busy thinking *She's so pretty, don't look at her, she's so pretty, don't look at her* to listen.

When the engines started up, I became incredibly nervous. Not because I thought we might crash or something, but because of what I might find—or not find—once we landed in Dubrovnik. It was a fourteen-hour flight, including fuel stops, so I had plenty of time to anticipate and speculate on what might lie ahead. I'd already waited two years since Vladimir Petrovic had appeared by our baby grand piano, so what was another fourteen hours?

Still, my mind raced with what-ifs: What if my real dad was alive? What if we found him lying in some hospital bed in a coma? Or what if I found out that he was healthy, except for the minor detail that he had no memory of his life before a bomb exploded on the bridge he was rebuilding? Or worse yet, what if he remembered everything but had chosen not to find me? What if seeing me only reminded him that he'd lost his wife and daughter, and he felt it would be best for both of us not to see each other? These thoughts were so intense that I didn't even realize the plane had taken off.

I looked at Robert sitting next to Larry and across from Cal, and my blood began to boil. If Robert had done anything to keep me from my real family, I would never forgive him.

As soon as our flight attendant announced we could "move about the cabin," I grabbed a pair of jeans and a T-shirt out of my travel bag and went to the bathroom to change.

When I returned to my seat, Cal was waiting for me.

"Hey, how's it going?" he said.

"Fine," I said cautiously.

"Great. Great," Cal said to all of us, running his bony fingers through his wavy black hair.

"Later on, we're going to get some footage of you talking about your expectations for the trip, your last memories, that sort of thing, you know, you know?" The double "you know" seemed to indicate that Cal was either naturally hyper or had drunk one too many espressos.

"His last memories are of his mother and sister being killed," Hana said disapprovingly, obviously having taken a disliking to Cal.

"Well, sure, sure," Cal responded, surprised to have been challenged. "I mean, that was just a figure of speech."

"His mother and sister being killed was a figure of speech?" Hana responded.

Cal looked at Tom and Jessica for help, but they just stared back at him blankly, letting him fry himself.

"No, no! What I meant . . . What I meant was . . . I'll be back later with my camera and my sound guy and we can do a little interview, that's all. Okay, great, great." And with that Cal made his way back up to where Robert, Larry, and the mini film crew were sitting.

"That was awesome," Martie said to Hana after Cal had left us.

"Where I come from, we say our opinions," Hana said.

"He was being a total idiot," Jessica said sharply.

"So, Joe, before the press conference Hana was telling us stories from when you were little," Tom said, a mischievous glint in his eyes. "And you made her out to be ancient. I was expecting an old lady using a walker to get around."

"Josef, I am only fifty-six," Hana said.

"Really?" I asked, making everyone laugh. In my memory, Hana had seemed so old, but I could see now I was wrong.

"Yes, really," Hana said, making me feel a little embarrassed.

"What did you tell them about me?" I asked, instantly regretting it.

"That you were always a wise guy, and stubborn, never taking a bath when I ask you to, and when I finally get you in the bath, I cannot get you out of the bath."

Greta appeared next to me. "You all seem to be enjoying yourselves," she said. "What are you talking about?"

"Josef not wanting to take a bath," Hana said.

"Oh, I love baths," Greta responded, instantly bringing the conversation to herself. "I can spend hours in the tub. When I get a new script, I make a big bubble bath, pour a glass of chardonnay, and start reading. Of course, I end up getting water and suds all over the script and it smears and I can't read half of it." Greta laughed; everyone else smiled politely. She cleared her throat. "Well, I think I'll go see when dinner is being served. I'm starving."

It was hard to think of America's favorite actress as an outsider, but that was what she'd just been. I sort of felt sorry for Greta, unable to fit in with our small group.

"This really was a great idea, Tom," she said, placing a hand on Tom's shoulder, a gesture that did not go unnoticed by Jessica. "I know this means a lot to Joe. I'm glad you're all with us," Greta said sincerely before walking toward the front of the plane.

"She's an odd one," Jessica said.

"What do you mean?" Tom asked.

"I mean, she can be so self-involved one moment and so sweet the next," Jessica answered.

"I wouldn't exactly say the next," I said. "More like a bunch of moments of being self-involved, then one of being sweet, then a bunch more of being into herself."

"You see?" Hana said. "A wise guy."

"And she's got a thing for you, Tom, I swear it," Jessica said.

"You're crazy," Tom said.

"I don't know," Jessica replied.

I was thinking that Jessica would be surprised to learn how hard Greta had been pushing Tom to propose to her.

We were scheduled to make two refueling stops along the way: one in New Jersey and the other in Paris. The leg of the flight that took us to New Jersey seemed to go quickly. After we'd been served dinner, I played Scrabble with Jessica and Martie. Tom was working on the book on his laptop, and Hana was sleeping.

"We should ask your sister and Greta if they want to play with us, too, don't you think?" Martie asked.

"I don't think they'd want to," I said.

"Greta looked like she wanted to be with us. I bet this

happens all the time. People think she doesn't want to do normal things just because she's a movie star. I think it's kind of a reverse snobbery. We assume she thinks she's better than us, but maybe it's the other way around. I'm going to ask them if they want to play," Martie said decisively, rising from her seat and walking up the aisle.

A few moments later, Martie returned with Greta and Guava.

"Told you," she whispered to me as Greta and Guava got their Scrabble tiles.

I smiled. She was right—again.

fifteen

We had just gotten back to our cruising altitude and speed after the refueling in New Jersey when Cal Noonan asked everyone to be quiet. He wanted to get some tape of Robert talking about the trip; my turn would come on the leg from Paris to Dubrovnik. Cal wanted us to be as close as possible to our destination before interviewing me.

I moved up the aisle, close enough to hear Robert speak.

Robert's appearance seemed to have changed simply because he'd announced he was running for public office. It was as if he'd put on a politician's mask, one whose strict lines of professional sincerity and righteousness had replaced the malleable lines of an actor.

"This is not my trip, this is Joe's trip," Robert said to Cal.

It was about the fifteenth time he'd made this statement since Tom suggested we go to Dubrovnik. "Joe is but one of the thousands of boys and girls who were made orphans by war in the Balkans. There are also over ten thousand children orphaned by wars in southern Africa, not to mention the children's lives that have been lost due to famine in Liberia and Sierra Leone. Only when we make children our number-one priority will we be—"

"Hold on," Larry said, stopping the interview.

"What?" said Robert.

"The orphans are in Liberia and Sierra Leone and the famine is in southern Africa," Larry said.

"Are you sure?" asked Robert.

I rolled my eyes and looked at Tom.

While Robert scanned his notes, I heard Larry say to Cal, "I smell an Oscar nomination." I nudged Tom, but he just shrugged in that *what can you do?* manner I'd come to know very well in the two months we'd been working on the book.

"Hana, tell us a little about where we're going," Tom asked.

"Did you know that Dubrovnik is called the pearl of the Adriatic?" Hana said to our little group.

Everyone said, "Yes."

"How did you know?" Hana asked.

"Google" was the chorused reply.

Even I'd learned more online about my home than I remembered from living there.

Everyone seemed to know that Dubrovnik was a beautiful

seaport city on the southern tip of what was called the Dalmatian Coast of the Adriatic Sea, north of the Mediterranean Sea and east of Italy.

"What they did to that beautiful city was inhuman and for no reason," Hana said.

"I read that there was no military presence there when they started bombing in 1992," Tom said.

"True," Hana said.

"Why did they bomb you, then?" Martie asked.

"I don't know. Everything was changing so fast. We wanted our independence. Why not? This was just before you were born, Josef. There was no water or electricity. There was an old Franciscan monastery with a well. In the morning we would go with our pails to fill them with water. I am sure your mother did this, too. There were no telephones, so we could not talk to our relatives to tell them we were all right. Can you imagine?"

"That must have been horrible," Jessica said.

"To take a bath we had to go into the ocean. It was December and the water was freezing, but it was the only way to get clean.

"There was one day," Hana went on, "when the bombing started in the early morning and did not end until late at night. It was December sixth. I never will forget that day.

"You know Dubrovnik is a very old city. It has been through many hardships but has always been beautiful. Many churches. Maybe they did not like our churches," Hana said, bittersweet.

"Another thing I read," said Tom, "was that the city used to be covered with red-tile roofs, but most of those were destroyed or damaged."

"I read they've fixed them," Martie said.

"Hana, how did you come to be Joe's nanny?" Jessica asked.

"My older brother was an army officer. He wanted me to be safe. My English was very good, and when Josef came to be taken by Mr. and Mrs. Francis, I was hired to come with them to America."

"Have you been back often?" Martie asked.

"Two times. The last time was two years ago. It is a very special place," Hana said with pride. "People from other parts of the country say that those of us from Dubrovnik think we are better than everyone else. It is not true. We are no better or worse. We are just from a better place." She winked at me.

Cal Noonan's interview with me began shortly after we'd taken off from Paris.

Before the filming started, Larry Weinstein prepped me.

"Just be yourself," he said. "Don't forget to say how grateful you are to your mom and dad for coming to your rescue. I like that, 'coming to your rescue.' Be sure to use that phrase."

"Got it," I said, fighting back the impulse to tell him to leave me alone.

"When Cal asks you what you're most looking forward to, say, 'Meeting the soldier who rescued me from that street.'"

"Do you want me to use *rescue* twice?" I asked with faked sincerity. Hana was right; I was a wise guy.

"Good point," said Larry. "Okay, well, you should use *rescue* for your mom and dad. How about *saved*? Yeah, that's good. The soldier who *saved* you during that battle or whatever was going on. If you say that Robert saved you, people might think you mean in a religious way. We don't want them to get that message. Not that your dad isn't supportive of people of faith."

Martie had come up behind Larry and was doing imitations of him as he gave me my instructions. When I started to laugh, Larry's antenna-like eyebrows picked up that something was going on behind him. But by the time he'd swung his neck around, all he found was Martie smiling innocently.

"And you need to change," Larry said, after turning back to face me.

I changed back into the clothes I had worn at Robert's press conference twelve hours before. Although almost everyone else had sacked out along the way, I had remained awake the whole time, too keyed up to sleep.

"Okay, Joe, don't look at the camera, look at me," Cal said seriously. "I'll ask you a question, but my voice will be cut out in editing, so try to incorporate my question into your answer." Cal and his minicrew had set up special lighting and clipped a microphone onto the collar of my shirt.

"For instance," Cal continued, "if I ask you, 'How long

has it been seen you've been in Dubrovnik?' you'll say, 'It's been twelve years since I've been to Dubrovnik.' "

"It's been ten years," I said.

"It has?" Cal said, looking down at a clipboard with scribbled notes on a pad. "Are you sure?"

"Yes," I said.

"You're fifteen, right?"

"I'm thirteen."

"Really?"

"Really."

I smell an Oscar nomination for Worst-Researched Documentary.

The interview continued in much this manner, with Cal asking me questions filled with false premises that I corrected when incorporating them into my answers:

"What was it like growing up as a Serb in Yugoslavia?"

"I'm Croatian. I wish I had had the opportunity to grow up in Croatia, but I was only three when I lost my family."

"Your real father was in the army, correct?"

"My father was an engineer. He was drafted into the army to rebuild bridges during the war."

"Would you like to be in the army someday?"

"I don't know," I said honestly. "The last thing I want to do is make more orphans."

"That was brilliant," Cal said, stopping the filming. "Ties right into your dad's—I mean, Robert's message. At least, I think it ties into Robert's message. Larry, what's Robert's message?"

"No more war orphans," Larry said from behind the *New York Times*.

"Exactly," Cal said.

"He has an amazing talent for bringing a picture together in post," Larry told Martie and me after the interview was concluded.

"What's post?" Martie asked.

"Postproduction," Larry said. "He's great at cutting segments together, adding music, film clips, photographs, finding the right actor to do the narration. All that."

Larry was pleased that I had gotten in everything he had told me to—about wanting to meet the soldier who had rescued me during the shelling on the day I'd lost my mother and sister, and how grateful I was to Robert and Greta for saving me from life in an orphanage. In truth, I *was* looking forward to meeting the soldier who had pulled me out of the street, and the ones who had taken me door to door in my old neighborhood. But more than that, I hoped I might find out what had happened to my father, and I clung to the remote possibility that, somehow, he might still be alive.

sixteen

My heartbeat sped up as I looked out my window and saw the deep blue waters of the Adriatic meeting the coastline of Croatia. Dubrovnik sat right on the coast, with the most ancient part of the city jutting out into the sea. The red-tile roofs that Hana had described formed a vision of my past and present. They had been repaired since I'd left the city, and you would never know they had been heavily bombarded a decade before.

Minutes later, our plane was on the runway. We taxied to a stop in front of a small group of buildings, including a tower with an octagonal control room.

No surprise—reporters, cameramen, and photographers were waiting for us as we descended the moveable stairway.

"Joe, how does it feel to be home?" a reporter shouted in Croatian as we walked to the limos that were waiting for us on the tarmac. Of course, I didn't understand a word he said, and it seemed ironic that Hana, who had originally been hired to translate English into Croatian for me, was now doing the opposite.

"It feels great," I said in English. Hana translated for the reporter, who seemed hurt that I hadn't answered in my native language.

"Mr. Francis," an attractive female reporter said, "do you think it will be an unfair advantage if *People* magazine names you its Sexiest Man Alive in an election year?"

"I think that's an *unfair* question," said Robert, laughing. "And by the way, not a position I'm campaigning for."

"Greta, rumor has it you're not too keen on your husband's running for the California Senate seat," a British journalist called out.

"Not true," Greta said with a smile. "I support whatever Robert does, same as he supports me. He'll make a great senator." *In public we are united* was Greta's motto.

Even Guava was asked a question by someone in the roped-off crowd.

"Guava, how do you think being a senator's daughter might affect your career?" a nasal voice called as we passed by. I wanted to laugh but thought it best not to; Martie, however, was not so generous. I caught her looking at Tom and Jessica, mouth agape.

"My CD will be out for Christmas," Guava hollered, staying on message as well as Robert or any other politician.

We split up into two limos, which exited the airport and were soon on the winding road that would lead us into Dubrovnik. When the city came into view, I was once again filled with hope and trepidation. Luckily, I was sitting next to Tom, who said, "Everything's going be fine." And then, "My God, that's a beautiful city."

We entered the city through one of its ancient gates, and everything looked both familiar and new.

Having Cal Noonan and his crew in my face as I took in my former home was distracting me from my having the sort of "true moment" that Cal was looking for. Still, seeing the brick buildings and marble streets in the city's Old Town, where our hotel was located, was remarkable.

Hana was greeted in the lobby of the hotel by her brother, and we made plans to reunite at dinner.

I roomed with Tom, while Martie stayed with Jessica. Robert and Greta had the nicest room in the hotel; Guava bunked with Megan in the room adjacent to theirs. Larry was the only person with a room to himself. Cal and his film crew were taken to another, cheaper hotel a distance from the center of the city.

"How does it feel to be back?" Tom asked once we were in our room.

"It's weird," I said, flopping down on my bed. "I feel like this is my first time here, too."

"Well, you were only three," Tom said, looking out the window to the square below. He then turned around to say, "I've been trying to figure out when we can go to Zagreb. It's a two-hour flight, and that doesn't include travel time to the airport and back, or to the Ministry of Defense. And then who knows how long it will take to talk to the right people who can tell us anything about your dad. Your schedule's jam-packed."

"Maybe we can stay an extra day," I said. "We can say we need to do some research there for the book. You know, about my dad and what he did in the army."

"Maybe," Tom said.

Tom must've been thinking that it would be best to tell Robert and Greta everything, because he got really quiet.

"What about Vladimir?" I asked. "Should we try to find him first? He might know something about my dad."

"I figure Jessica and I can take part of tomorrow to call every Vladimir Petrovic listed in the phone book. If he's here, we'll find him," Tom said confidently. He looked out the window again. "Let's get Jessica and Martie and go for a walk," he said, brightening.

A few hours later we gathered for dinner at a restaurant Megan had chosen because it specialized in vegetarian and seafood dishes, which complied with Robert's and Greta's food regimens. The restaurant was walking distance from our hotel, next to a set of steps leading up to an old Catholic church—the city was crazy with old churches. Our table was outside on the plaza, which looked spectacular at night, the yellow brick buildings and marble street lit by lanterns attached to the buildings.

We would have probably gone unnoticed by the other diners and passersby had Cal not been hovering close by with a digital video camera, documenting such monumental moments as our taking a spoonful of soup or a bite of fresh fish.

I sat next to Tom, who was next to Jessica, and across from Martie. I was exhausted from lack of sleep and nervous anticipation of what I might or might not find. It was still hard to believe I was home, and more than ever, the images I had mentally carried all these years seemed like movies that had been shown to me over and over again rather than real memories.

Guava was sitting on my other side. At one point she looked up at me, smiled, and said, "I like your city."

"Thanks," I said. "I like it, too."

"Mommy said that Cal can film me dancing here and we can put it in the video for my CD."

"That would be nice," I said.

"You can be in it if you want."

Guava was definitely her mother's daughter, her generosity firmly attached to her own self-interest. Still, whether from lack of sleep or because at that moment I was riding a hope wave, there was something about her offer that touched me. Maybe Martie was right; maybe, in my own way, I'd been a snob to Guava.

"Sure," I said, "that would be cool. Maybe you could even shoot some of it on those steps."

"That would be awesome. I'm going to ask Mommy." Guava turned to Greta and excitedly said, "Mommy, Mommy," until Greta turned and faced her.

Greta smiled with delight as Guava told her about shooting her dancing on the nearby steps.

Despite all Greta's faults, one thing was clear: she loved Guava. I suddenly got very sad looking at them. A chickpea striking me on the temple snapped me out of it.

"What are you thinking about?" Martie asked.

"Nothing," I said. It had been a while since I had lost my voice while looking into Martie's eyes, but in the lamplight of the plaza I found myself once again unable to form words in my brain, let alone get them out of my mouth. I spotted the bread basket, grabbed a piece, and focused on buttering it. My brain and throat loosened a bit.

"Is it hard with your mom . . . ?" I wasn't sure how to finish the sentence.

"Acting like a teenager?" Martie said. "Yeah, it's really hard. Luckily, I have Jessica. I don't know what I'd do without her. But I know my mom loves me. She's never left me alone. She always makes sure there's someone with me when she's acting like an idiot over some stupid guy."

I couldn't get any more butter on my bread, so I looked

up at Martie. I wanted to say something nice or comforting but couldn't come up with anything.

"What?" she asked.

I shrugged and took a bite of heavily buttered bread.

"You're cute when you're nervous," Martie said, biting her lip.

"I'm what?" I said, choking on the bread and starting to cough.

"Are you okay?"

"I'm fine," I said, finally getting the hunk of bread down.

I was feeling a warm sensation in my face. *I must be turning red,* I thought, *but why am I only turning red on the right side of my face?* I turned and found myself looking into Cal Noonan's handheld camera.

"Just keep acting normal," Cal said.

Normal! There was nothing normal about anything that was going on. I was in a city that was more foreign than familiar; my adoptive father, who was sitting a few feet away, had kept information from me about my real father; and a girl I had a crush on had just told me I was cute.

"Can you wait till after we've eaten?" Tom said, coming to my aid.

"Well, no, not really," Cal said, somewhat offended. "The point of the documentary is to document what you're doing . . . while you're doing it."

If that sounded as ridiculous to Tom as it did to me, he didn't let on. Instead, he very calmly said, "I understand, but it's been a long day, and it would be nice for Joe to have a few moments without the camera on him. Have you had something to eat yet?"

"Not really," Cal said, lowering the camera. "There's so much I want to get. I'm just serving the needs of the film."

"Well, take a break and pull up a chair," Tom said, "and serve yourself some of this great food."

"I *am* kind of hungry," Cal said.

Tom motioned for the waiter, and Cal took a seat at the end of the table and began picking at the various appetizers that were laid out in front of him.

" 'The point of a documentary is to document what you're doing,' " Martie whined in a deep voice, quietly imitating Cal.

"Shh," Jessica said.

"He can't hear me," Martie replied.

"Save it for later," Jessica said.

"Okay," Martie said. She then turned to me and said, "I don't think I'd want to be a celebrity."

"I'm not a celebrity," I grumbled, as if she'd called me a jerk.

"You sort of are. Anyway, what I'm saying is, I wouldn't want cameras shoved in my face all the time and reporters and people asking me stuff that was none of their business."

I smiled. Martie understood what life in the spotlight was like for me, and that made me feel good.

Tom and I entered the hotel ahead of the others. We saw Vladimir Petrovic immediately, walking toward us, his eyes glistening. He looked the same as he had a couple of years before, although there may have been a few more gray hairs in his bushy mustache.

"Josef," he said, grabbing me by the shoulders.

"Mr. Petrovic," I said, astonished that the man I'd been wondering about for two years was now standing beside me.

"Vladimir, Vladimir, please."

"Um, Vladimir," Tom said, "we should go somewhere"—Tom looked over his shoulder to see if anyone was coming—"else."

"This is Tom," I said. "He's helping me write a book."

"It is my pleasure to meet you," Vladimir said, enthusiastically shaking Tom's hand.

I heard people approaching the hotel entrance.

"Come on," Tom said. He rushed us past the front desk, down a hallway, around a corner, and through a back exit.

"Mr. Francis, is he still a problem for me?" Vladimir said once we were outside.

"For both of us," I said.

"I do not know why he makes such problems when none are there." Vladimir's eyes then started to glisten again. "Josef, you are so tall. You look just like your mother."

His words made me feel warm inside. Here was a man with a direct connection to my parents. Someone who'd known them and could see them in me.

"How did you know where we were?" Tom asked.

"When I hear you are in Dubrovnik, I ask around. I am very happy. I know many people in the hotel business. I manage little hotel outside of city. Very nice hotel. Everyone in Dubrovnik is in the tourist business. It's not so good right after war, but very good now."

I had so many questions for Vladimir, I didn't know where to start. I was thankful when Tom asked, "How did you know Joe's family?"

"My brother was married to your father's sister," Vladimir said. "I see you as a very little boy many times."

"Do you know what happened to my father?" I asked.

Vladimir looked confused. "What do you mean?" he said.

I told him about the letter that had been sent to my mother saying that my father was not dead, as they had previously reported, but missing in action.

Vladimir nodded as I spoke, his eyes once again getting watery, but this time not from happiness.

"It cannot be. Everyone who survived returned after the war. I am sorry for you, Joe," Vladimir said sadly.

"But what if he had amnesia and didn't remember who he was?" I said, still holding on to a glimmer of hope.

"I do not think so, but relations are still not so good between countries who fought the war. Other families have same problem."

"What happened when you came to see Joe in Los Angeles?" Tom asked, changing the subject.

"Did Robert get you thrown out of the country?" I added.

"No, no. I come to L.A. to visit you, Joe."

This made me feel worse than ever that Robert had kept him from seeing me.

"Robert said he bribed you to stay away from me," I said.

"What is this?" Vladimir asked, confused.

"Paid you money not to see me."

"No, no, no," Vladimir said emphatically. "I write to you to tell you I am coming, and you do not write back, but I think, Okay, he's a boy, is typical. When I come to your home first time, I am taken away. When I come to your home second time, I am taken away but told to meet with your father and someone else."

"Larry, his lawyer," I said.

"Right. Larry say, 'How much do you want to go away?'"

"I say, 'I do not want to go away, I want to see Josef. I come to see Josef.' I say, 'I want to take him maybe to Disneyland.' Larry say again, 'How much do you want?' I think he wants to give me money for me to take you to Disneyland. I know it costs much and I am not rich, so I say, 'Maybe one hundred dollars? This is very nice of you.' He writes me check for one hundred twenty dollars. I leave. Then I come to your house on your birthday and am thrown away," Vladimir said, still hurt by what had happened.

"Wow," Tom said. "They thought they'd bought you off for a hundred and twenty bucks. Unbelievable."

"Maybe I should not have taken. But I hear that Disney is expensive land. I have not so much money as I do now. Later, I send the check back to Larry."

"That must be the letter Larry told Rusty about," Tom

said. "You weren't in jail, were you?" Tom asked, bringing up Robert's other justification for keeping Vladimir out of our house and my life.

"Jail? No, never," he said, a little insulted.

"I figured," Tom said.

Hearing Vladimir confirm what I had suspected all along caused me to well up with anger at Robert and Larry for having treated him so badly.

"Joe, I want to throw a big party for you the night after the next night. Friends of your mother and father will come to see you, yes?"

"I want to, but they plan everything I do," I said with bitterness.

"We'll work it out," Tom said.

"And tell your newer father and mother to come too. I keep no hard feelings. They did what they thought best for you."

I found that difficult to believe. Best for them was more like it.

"We'd better get back inside," Tom said. "They'll be wondering where we are."

Vladimir handed Tom and me his card. The hotel he managed was called the Pearl. "You can reach me here. Call if you need anything. Anything at all. I'll see you in two nights. Come at eight o'clock. Okay?"

Vladimir gave each of us one more suffocating bear hug before turning and walking away down the narrow street behind our hotel.

seventeen

The soldier who had pulled me out of the street ten years before was easy to find. He was still living in Dubrovnik and working in the tourist industry, just like Vladimir.

His name was Andro, and he gave tours for a living. He was around thirty years old and was dressed in black slacks and a white short-sleeved shirt.

"He's perfect," Cal Noonan said, as if Andro were an actor who'd auditioned for the part of himself.

We were outside the old city in the neighborhood I had lived in for the first three years of my life. The street Andro had pulled me from a decade before had been closed off for our meeting. Besides Cal and the two-man crew he'd brought with him from Los Angeles, there were several additional local camera and crew people. A surprisingly large press contingency was also on hand.

Larry Weinstein and Cal choreographed everything. First I was to walk into the street by myself and look around; then, after several minutes, Andro would come into the street and we would shake hands.

"Why can't they let you be natural?" Hana asked.

"It's like reality television," I said. "They script everything for the most impact."

"*Survivor* is scripted?" Hana was aghast.

"Pretty much," I said.

"Did you hear that, Luka?" Hana said, turning to her brother.

"What is *Survivor*?" her brother asked.

I didn't know what shocked Hana more: that her favorite reality show might be scripted or that her brother had never heard of it.

"Okay, Joe," Cal said. "We're all set. Don't forget to look around and take in all the buildings. Anytime you're ready." Cal moved away and took his position next to a small monitor that showed what each of the cameras was filming.

"This is so stupid," Martie said. "Why can't you just go and meet him?"

I looked across the street to where Robert, Greta, and Guava were seated in directors' chairs. Later, they'd get their chance to thank Andro, and pictures would be taken that would appear in newspapers all over the world, maybe not on the front page like ten years ago, but prominently enough, considering Robert's announced candidacy for the Senate. Andro was standing a few feet from Robert. Cal had decided it was best to keep Andro and me from saying anything to each other until we were face to face in the middle of the street. "Save it for the camera," Cal had said.

"Anytime, Joe," Cal called from ten feet away.

My feet were frozen to the pavement. This *was* stupid. Why did every moment in my life have to be staged and manipulated for some other purpose?

"Joe, did you hear him?" Jessica said softly.

I nodded.

Cal walked over to me. "Is there a problem?" he asked.

"I'm not going out there," I said

"What do you mean you're not going out there?" Cal asked. "We've got a scene to shoot."

"I'm not going to be in your scene," I said, seeing no need to explain myself.

"It's not my scene, kid. It's yours."

Robert was walking across the street toward me. "What's going on?" he said.

"I don't want to do it."

"You don't want to meet the man who rescued you?" Robert said reproachfully, his tone implying I was an ungrateful little snot.

"I don't want to meet him like this."

"Just do it," Robert said firmly.

"No," I said just as firmly.

The press had caught wind that something was amiss and began moving in on us.

"You're embarrassing me and you're embarrassing yourself. Tom, tell him to go into the street."

"It's up to him," Tom said.

Robert gave Tom a *how dare you? you work for me* glare.

"Give us a minute," Tom said.

"All right," Robert said, "but this better end with Joe walking into that street." He motioned to the press to back off, saying, "It's all right. This is very emotional for him."

"I'm proud of you," Tom said. "That took guts. But we've got a lot more to do. We came here to find out about your dad. So I think you should forget about Robert and forget about what Cal told you. Just go out there and wait for Andro. Cal's not going to direct you when you get out there, not with all these reporters around. Just meet Andro and forget everything else that's going on."

"Okay," I said, calming down. I knew Tom was right.

I walked into the street. In my peripheral vision I could see Cal scrambling to get his crew moving, but I pushed them out of my mind. I was determined not to think about the last time I stood in this spot, because that was what Cal and Robert and Larry wanted: an emotional moment showing Joe, the orphan boy, remembering how he lost his mother and sister. After a few minutes Andro stepped off the curb and walked toward me.

"Hello, Josef," he said. Upon closer look, Andro seemed older than his thirty years.

"Hi," I said back to him.

"You look good," Andro said, putting a hand on my shoulder. "A fine-looking young man. You will have lots of girlfriends, I am sure." He laughed.

For a moment I thought about Martie, but then I refocused.

"Thanks for saving me," I said.

"You are most welcome," he said. "Please call me if you need anything. I have the best tour in the city. I know the old city and the countryside."

"Okay," I said. "That would be great."

Then we shook hands—not because Cal and Robert and Larry wanted me to, but because it felt right.

The next item on our itinerary was a trip to the historic stone wall that encircled the city. Robert hadn't spoken to me since our confrontation earlier that morning. Greta had given me a conspiratorial wink when we left Andro. I wasn't sure what was behind it; it might have simply been her pleasure at seeing Robert take one on the nose, or it might have been respect for my defiance of him. Maybe it was a little of both. Jessica had said, "I think she wants to be your friend."

We were on the westernmost side of the wall, the Adriatic Sea shimmering beneath us on one side and the red-tile

rooftops stretching out on the other. While Cal was busy filming Robert being interviewed by a woman from a local newspaper, the rest of us had a chance to act like real tourists, taking
pictures of ourselves in every combination: Tom and me, Jessica
and Martie, me with Greta and Guava, and so on. It was funny;
seeing Greta and Guava through the eyes of Martie, Jessica,
and Tom made me feel closer to them.

The same couldn't be said of my feelings toward Robert.

When the reporter had finished speaking to him, Robert
left to go back to the hotel for another interview without saying a word to me. Under Larry's supervision, I began my interview with the woman from the newspaper. Cal and his camera
crew were stationed nearby. The reporter spoke English, so I
didn't need Hana to translate. I was still feeling defiant, so I
answered each of her questions, paying no heed to the carefully prepared statements Larry had gone over with me.

"Josef, how does it feel to be home?"

"It's strange. I'm happy to be here, but I don't exactly feel
like it's my home anymore."

"Do you think of Los Angeles as your home?"

"No, not really. It's complicated."

"You were adopted by two of the most famous actors in
the world. What has that been like for you?"

I could see Larry tensing up about ten feet away from me.
His hands were in his pockets, maybe to prevent himself
from running over to choke me if I said the wrong thing.

"It's weird. I mean, what do you think?"

"I think it could be quite entertaining," the reporter said.

"It's that, all right," I said. "But it's hard to . . . just be."

I wondered how long it would be before Larry stopped the interview.

"What do you mean?" she asked pointedly, clearly realizing that this wasn't going to be the fluff interview she'd expected.

"Sometimes it feels like one big commercial. Someone is always promoting something, and we have to be so careful about what we say because it can get misinterpreted, or correctly interpreted, and lead to trouble."

Larry was shaking his head disapprovingly out of the reporter's view. I ignored him.

"I understand you are writing a book. Will you tell the truth in it, as you are now?"

"Yes," I said, knowing my answer might come back to haunt me.

"How would you rate Robert Francis and Greta Powell as parents?"

"Okay, we really need to wrap this up here," Larry cut in. "We've got an extremely tight schedule today, and we're already behind."

"But this is great stuff," Cal said, filming Larry as he spoke. Cal was obviously more loyal to getting good material on film than he was to Robert or Larry.

"Turn that thing off," Larry said.

"Why?" Cal asked. My defiance seemed to have spread to our documentarian.

The reporter was jotting down their exchange as quickly as she could write.

"Turn it off," Larry said again, walking toward Cal, who backed away, keeping his camera going the whole time.

Larry put his hand over the camera and tried to take it out of Cal's hands. The others in our group kept their distance, but now I saw Tom rushing to help. He arrived just a moment too late as Cal, jerking his camera away, caused Larry to fall backward down a set of stone steps. Larry went tumbling like a bowling pin, finally coming to a stop on the landing about fifteen steps below.

"Aaahhhh!" Larry groaned loudly.

"What happened?" Tom said as we ran down the steps.

"I told the truth," I said, reaching Larry.

Hearing the word *truth*, Larry let out another "Aaahhh!"

eighteen

"How could you do this to your uncle Larry?" Robert asked me. We were with Greta and Tom in our hotel's restaurant, which was closed between lunch and dinner.

"He's not my uncle and I didn't do anything to him," I said.

Robert looked at me like he didn't know who I was.

"How is he?" I asked.

"He broke his right leg and his left thumb," Robert said.

"At least he can still write checks," I said flippantly.

Greta looked like she was holding back a laugh.

"That's not funny," Robert said sternly to all of us. "He wouldn't have gotten hurt if you had done as you were told."

"I'm sorry he got hurt," I said, "but it's not my fault.

"You're making things very difficult for everybody. You're being selfish."

Of all the people to tell me I was being selfish, Robert seemed the least qualified. Or maybe the most, since he was an expert at it.

"Larry said you told the reporter that you wanted to tell the truth in your book. Is that right?" Robert asked.

"Yes," I said, regretting that I had told the truth about telling the truth.

"Well, I'm not sure what you mean by that, but I assume that there is more to what you've written so far than we've seen. Is that right, Tom?"

"There is," Tom said uneasily. "I thought it would be best to include that material when we were finished. So you could see everything in context."

I looked at Greta. She no longer seemed amused.

Robert was shaking his head disapprovingly. "Tom, I want to see all your files for the book. You can put them on a CD and give it to Megan." He looked at his watch and stood. "I have a conference call in a few minutes. We'll talk again later," he said, indicating that we were dismissed.

Tom and I started to get up. "I have a few things to say," Greta said, remaining firmly in her chair.

"Of course," Robert said, realizing that he had left Greta out of the conversation.

Tom and I sat back down. Robert gave me one last *you're in big trouble, mister* look before walking away.

"I can't believe you deceived me like that," Greta said,

sounding more hurt than angry. "I can understand your not wanting to tell Robert. He can be such a control freak. But what could you possibly have written that you thought would upset me?"

A lot of stuff.

"And, Tom, I thought I could trust you. We've had such good talks."

"I'm sorry, Greta. Joe's gone through so much, and he's been very open about how he feels. Amazingly open for someone his age." Tom looked over at me. "Like I was saying before, I wanted you to see everything in context."

"Am I that horrible that I need to see things in context?" Greta said.

"That's not what I mean," Tom said.

"Fine. We'll read what you've put together thus far, and we'll take it from there," Greta said, all businesslike. She then became reflective. "I've tried to love both my children equally. I'm sorry you don't see that, Joe."

"What do you think Robert will do when he reads it?" I asked Tom when we were back in our room.

"I don't know. Probably fire me. It's happened before."

For the first time, I didn't feel bad just for myself. I felt bad for Tom, too. I thought about what he'd once said to me: that he was a professional failure, never quite making it to the majors in anything he did. Even writing this book with me, a book he'd never even get his name on the cover of, was turning into a failure for him.

"Does this mean the trip to Zagreb is off?" I asked Tom.

Tom set down the brush he'd been using on his thinning hair. "I promised we'd find out what happened to him, and we will."

"Okay," I said, hopeful but not exactly reassured. "I guess I messed things up by saying what I did to that reporter."

"No. Don't worry about it. And as for Larry, he made his own bed."

"A hospital bed, in this case," I joked.

"So what do we have going on tonight?"

"A concert," I said.

"What kind?"

"Folk music. And dancing. This place is crazy with folk dancing."

"Hana and her brother are about to get on the plane," Tom said to me after hanging up the phone the next morning. He had formulated his plan during the longest folk music and dance program in the history of the world.

Hana and Luka were going to the Ministry of Defense in Zagreb, which was two hundred miles away, to see if they could find any information about my father. If anyone asked why Hana wasn't with me, we'd say she was feeling ill.

My expectations were low, especially after having talked

to Vladimir on our first night in Dubrovnik, still clutching my glimmer of hope.

We were about to go down to breakfast when the phone rang; it was Vladimir with some very interesting news. One of the other hotel managers in the part of Dubrovnik where Vladimir worked had reported that Cal and his crew had checked out of their hotel that morning.

"Josef, tonight is going to be very special," Vladimir said in his rough voice. "People will be happy to see you all grown up."

"I want to meet them, too," I said.

"And remember what I told you. Bring your new parents. They are welcome."

"Um, okay," I said, not wanting to try to explain how unlikely that was.

After hanging up the phone, I said, "Do you think Robert fired Cal because he kept filming me when Larry told him to stop?"

"I don't know. Could be."

There was a knock on the door. It was Megan, there to pick up the CD with all Tom's book files on it.

"How are you doing, Megan?" Tom said while rummaging through his bag for the CD.

"Robert's asking me to do all this stuff for him with Larry laid up."

"How is Larry?" Tom asked.

"Pretty out of it. It's the thumb that's giving him a lot of pain. I wish I could have seen it." Megan smiled mischievously.

Tom handed the CD to Megan.

"I can't wait to read it," she said with a twinkle in her eye. "All right, see you guys later."

Tom and I went to breakfast with Jessica and Martie in the hotel restaurant while, I supposed, Robert and Greta were upstairs reading *all* the pages Tom had written thus far.

I wondered how Greta would feel about some of the things I had said about her. She'd probably feel hurt. I suddenly felt bad about the way I'd portrayed her.

While we waited for our food, we told Jessica and Martie what we'd learned about Cal.

"What are we doing today?" Martie asked.

"Key to the city," I said, reading my itinerary.

"You're getting a key to the city?" Jessica asked.

"The mayor is supposed to give it to me at one of the gates into the city."

"Sounds like something Larry must have arranged," Tom said.

"How is he, anyway?" Jessica asked.

"Larry? He's back here at the hotel, but I doubt he'll be getting around much," Tom said.

"After I get the key, Robert's supposed to make a little speech," I said.

"What about this afternoon?" Martie asked as the waiter set our breakfast in front of us.

"This afternoon's free. Tomorrow we're supposed to go to the cemetery where my mom and sister are buried." I poked at my waffle for a few seconds. "I don't think I want to go. I mean, not with all those cameras around."

"I've got an idea," Tom said with a sparkle in his eye.

★ ★ ★

As soon as the key-to-the-city presentation ended, Guava gave me a big hug and a "congratulations."

Greta also hugged me. "I'm sorry I got angry with you last night."

"That's okay," I said, relieved.

"I've decided to take Tom's advice and wait until you're finished to read your book. It's going to be a challenge for me, but I think it's the right thing to do. We're in this together," she said sweetly.

"Thank you," I said, surprised and moved by her words. "Are you going to stay and hear Robert's speech?"

"Are you kidding?" Greta laughed. "We've got shopping to do, don't we, honey," she said to Guava.

"I want a dress like the ones those ladies we saw dancing last night had," Guava said excitedly.

"We'll see you later," Greta said as Guava took hold of her hand and pulled her away.

"Greta," I called, running after her. "Do you and Guava want to come with us to the cemetery?"

"That's tomorrow, honey."

"I wanted to go when there wouldn't be so many people and cameras around. Tom arranged it."

"I'm sure he did," Greta said. "You two." She paused for a moment. "Thank you for inviting me. It means a great deal to me that you did." Greta looked like she was about to cry. "But I think you need to do this on your own. That was the point, wasn't it?"

I shrugged. "Don't tell Robert about it, okay?"

"About what?" Greta smiled.

Tom had arranged for Andro to take us to the cemetery. It was a few miles outside the city, and Andro pointed out landmarks, in true tour-guide fashion, as he worked his way onto the coastal route. It was another gorgeous, warm summer day. On one side of the road was the beautiful blue sea, while cypress trees covered the hills on the other side.

After a few minutes, we cut back inland through an old village. On the outskirts of the village was a gravel road that led to the Catholic church and cemetery where my mother and sister were buried. We passed through a white wrought-iron gate. There were many old—in some cases, crumbling—gravestones, shaded by mandarin orange, date palm, and olive trees, among others. The abundant trees provided shade for the entire cemetery.

We had just gotten out of Andro's van when a thin, middle-aged priest began walking toward us from the rectory.

He spoke only Croatian, so Andro did the talking for our little group.

The priest told Andro that he had been expecting us the next day, but he seemed unfazed by our early arrival.

We followed him across the grounds; there were gravestones dating as far back as the sixteenth century. There were chipped statues of saints, some without arms, other missing noses or even their whole heads.

Andro pointed to one of the statues and said, "That is Saint Blasius. He is the patron saint of Dubrovnik."

"What did he do?" asked Martie.

"He was beheaded." Andro said flatly, as if that alone qualified him for sainthood.

"Why is he a saint?" asked Jessica.

"One story says he was a doctor who became a bishop and he cured a young boy who had a fishbone stuck in his throat," Andro explained.

"Those can be nasty," Tom said. "I caught one of those in my throat at dinner the other night."

"That was when it was not good to be a Christian," Andro continued. "And to do anything that might be thought of as miraculous. So, the Romans took off his head. Same old story, you hear all the time."

The priest led us to some gravestones beneath an olive tree. There were markers for my mother and sister along with ones for my grandmother and grandfather on my mother's side of the family. They had lived in the nearby village but had died many years before I was born.

"We'll give you some time alone," Tom said. "Take as long as you need."

"Thanks," I said, looking at my friends. "But stay close by, okay?"

"Whatever you need," Tom said reassuringly.

I looked at the graves of my mother and sister. For the first time since we had arrived in Dubrovnik, I truly felt like I was home. I had seen their graves when they had been buried ten years earlier, but this time was different. I stared at the headstones, feeling a slight breeze from the nearby ocean on my face. The images of my mother and sister appeared before me—and my dad was with them. I wanted to make his image go away. I wanted him to be alive somewhere, waiting for *me* to appear before *him*. But he stayed where he was: with them, his arm around my mother's waist and his hand resting gently on my sister's shoulder.

nineteen

Andro dropped us off at the entrance to the old city that was closest to our hotel. When I got out of the van, I invited Andro to come to Vladimir's party that evening. They were the first words I'd spoken since we'd left the cemetery. The image of my family had remained vivid in my mind on the drive back.

"I will bring my wife and little boy," Andro said. "He is the same age as you were the last time we met."

When we got back to the hotel, Robert was seated alone in the lobby reading the *New York Times*.

"We'll go upstairs," Jessica said, leaving Tom and me to face Robert.

We walked over to where he was seated.

"I haven't been ditched since high school," Robert said. He set down his paper and stood up. "There's a little café just down the street we can go to. Greta will join us when she gets back. Gregor," Robert said to the tall, thin desk clerk with his head shaved. "Can you please tell Ms. Powell that we're at the café a couple of doors down?"

"I certainly will, Mr. Francis," the clerk said politely.

Robert, the true politician, knew most of the hotel staff's names, along with some bit of personal information he could chat with them about.

"Gregor is studying to be a marine biologist," Robert said as we walked out the front entrance.

I was sure Gregor was a great guy and would make a super marine biologist, but at the moment, he wasn't all that important to me.

"This really is an amazing place," Robert said. "Did you know that when George Bernard Shaw came here, he wrote: 'Those who seek paradise on Earth should come to Dubrovnik and see Dubrovnik'?"

"Did Greta tell you where we were?" I asked as we walked down the street.

"She did, but don't be angry with her. She did it for a good reason."

"What reason?" I said, feeling a little betrayed.

"Why don't we wait until she gets here. What was it like for you when you went to the cemetery?"

"It was hard," I said.

"I'm sure it was."

"It was my idea," said Tom.

I stopped walking, causing Robert and Tom to do the same. "You can't fire Tom," I pleaded.

"Who said anything about firing Tom?" Robert looked genuinely surprised at my assumption.

"You fired Cal because he didn't do what Larry told him to do," I said, "and now you're going to fire Tom because of what we've written about you and Greta in the book."

"Joe, I didn't fire Cal because of what happened yesterday. Well, maybe I did, but not for the reason you're thinking. After everything that happened yesterday I realized that I was ruining this experience for you. . . . Why don't we sit down in the café over here and talk, okay?"

We walked a little further and sat at a table outside of a small café. Robert and Tom ordered beers and I ordered a Coke.

Once we were settled in, Robert said, "I let Cal go because I finally listened to you. You didn't want a bunch of cameras and microphones in your face. I'm sorry it took me so long to get the message."

I was stunned to hear Robert make this confession. "Thank you," I said after a few minutes. And then I felt like revealing something truthful to him. "The year before last I found the letter about my father."

"I know," Robert said.

"You knew? Why didn't you say anything? Why didn't you do anything?" I said angrily.

"I just found out this afternoon. Hana called me."

"Hana?"

"Here's your mother," Robert said, looking relieved, as Greta approached us.

"Hey there," she said, a little too brightly, before taking a seat between Tom and Robert. I could tell that something wasn't right and she was compensating with good cheer.

"What's going on?" I asked. "What did Hana tell you?"

"Hana called me from Zagreb this afternoon," Robert slowly explained. "She was very upset—you know how Hana can get. She told me you knew that your father had been reported missing in action, and that she'd gone with her brother to find out what happened."

"You should have told us, honey," Greta said, reaching across the table and taking my hand. "We thought it was best not to say anything. We didn't want to get your hopes up."

I pulled my hand away. "Did you even try?" I asked harshly. "Did you try to find out what happened to him?"

"We did everything we could think of," Robert said calmly. "I talked to everyone I knew in Washington, but it was always the same answer: no. The Yugoslavian government, the Serbs, the Croatians, and other countries involved in the Balkan wars were still withholding information on MIAs for their own purposes."

"Until recently," Greta said, her eyes starting to water.

"What happened?" I asked, my voice tense.

"Well," Robert resumed, "what Hana and her brother found out this afternoon was that an agreement was recently reached between all the parties to, among other things, release information on MIAs." Robert took a deep breath. "They wouldn't give any specific information to Hana because she wasn't a relative . . . so she called me. I immediately called our embassy in Zagreb, and they were able to get the defense ministry to release the information about your father."

"What did they find out?" I asked, knowing and dreading the answer.

"Your dad died on August third, just inside the Croatian-Serbian border. He was buried there along with other Croatian soldiers. I'm sorry, Joe."

What I had known in my heart at the cemetery I finally knew to be true in fact: my father was gone and he would never come back, nor would any other member of my real family.

Greta, who was now sobbing, came around the table and hugged me.

I looked at Tom, who had placed a hand on my shoulder. "I know," he said. "I know."

Robert put his hand on my other shoulder. I didn't mind. I was glad he was there. The four of us stayed that way for a long time.

The rest of the afternoon was kind of foggy. I know we went back to the hotel and ended up in Robert and Greta's room, where we were joined by Jessica, Martie, and Guava. I know we played Scrabble on the bed, but I can't exactly remember who was playing. I know Tom left to take a walk with Jessica around sunset.

Tom must've told Robert about the party that evening at Vladimir's hotel, because after he left, Robert said, "I'm sorry I messed up things with this Vladimir fellow. I was rash trying to protect you. I'm so used to people wanting things from me."

"He wasn't in jail," I said.

"I know. I've already run into two other Vladimir Petrovics since we've been here," Robert said with a little laugh. "Larry and I were idiots. I'm sorry."

Hearing him say he was sorry and had been wrong about Vladimir caused any resentment I was still feeling toward Robert to slip away.

After a while Tom and Jessica came back into the room. Both were smiling, and it didn't take me long to figure out why: Jessica had an engagement ring on her finger.

"Congratulations." I said, shaking Tom's hand.

"Thanks. When it came down to it, that was pretty easy."

"It's so pretty," Martie said, examining Jessica's outstretched hand.

"Let me see, let me see!" Guava yelled.

"So you finally stepped up to the plate," Greta teased Tom.

"Yep, probably jinxed the whole thing," Tom said.

"I don't think so. You two will be together forever," Greta said. She looked over at Robert, who was already gazing at her.

"What?" she said to him.

"Nothing," Robert said, but the way they were looking at each other made me feel like they, too, had been changed by the day's events.

twenty

That evening all of us, even Larry in his leg and thumb casts, went to Vladimir's hotel, the Pearl.

Andro and his family were there, along with twenty or thirty people I didn't recognize who had known my father and mother, or were friends of Vladimir.

Robert apologized to Vladimir, who generously said, "I hold no hard feelings."

When Hana and her brother, Luka, arrived, I immediately thanked them for helping find out about my father.

"I didn't know what to do, so I called your other father," Hana said. "He is a good man."

I was beginning to see that what Hana was saying was true. Robert had helped me to learn the truth about my father, and he'd done it without making it about himself, or his run for the Senate, or any other reason than that it was right for me. Not only that, but on Greta's advice, he had decided to wait until we were finished with the book before reading it—a very un-Robert-like thing to do. Just when you think you know a person, they surprise you.

As for Greta, now that she had successfully needled Tom into proposing to Jessica, she was focusing on needling me into telling Martie I liked her.

"You're turning red. You look like that punch you're holding," Greta teased.

"Greta, stop it," I said.

"Well, if you don't tell her, maybe I will," Greta said, feigning a move toward Martie.

"No!" I protested, a little too vigorously, causing Greta to laugh.

"Maybe when we get back home," I said.

"Excellent," Greta said victoriously. "I'll tell you exactly what to say and how and where to say it. I'm thinking the gazebo."

"Fine," I said dismissively, but actually happy to have her help.

We were interrupted by a trio of men who said they knew my family, but I think they really just wanted to meet Greta.

I left them with her and wandered over to where Tom, Jessica, and Martie were standing.

"What was Greta saying to you?" Martie asked. "You were all red."

"Nothing," I said, willing my face to stay its normal color.

Luckily, Robert walked up to us. "I invited Vladimir to come to L.A. and stay with us," he said.

"Really? That's great," I said happily. I looked at Tom, who seemed to be as pleased as I was. Something suddenly occurred to me. "Can Tom have his name on the book?"

"What?" Robert said, not following me.

"Can the book say, 'by Josef Francis, with Tom Dolan'?"

"That's nice of you, Joe," Tom said, "but the contract says—"

"Say no more," Robert said. "Done."

"Thanks," Tom said to Robert and me.

"No problem," I said, knowing we wouldn't be standing here in Dubrovnik without his help.

"Daddy, Joe, come here!" Guava shouted from the other side of the room. She was standing with Greta and a woman with a small digital camera.

"Shall we?" Robert asked.

While walking across the room, I spotted Martie and Jessica standing with Hana. "Come on," I said. "You guys should be in the picture, too."

Before we could get ourselves organized for the photo, Vladimir tapped his glass with a fork and asked everyone to be quiet in both English and Croatian. "I would like everyone to raise their glasses," Vladimir said. He then looked at me. "Josef, we are so happy that you returned to your home, and proud to see what a fine young man you are. To Josef."

Everyone toasted me, and I felt their warmth. I looked at these people I'd just met, and at Vladimir, who had tried so hard to meet me once before and was now throwing me this party; I looked at Robert, Greta, and Guava, holding their glasses up to me, and I thought that no matter how many movies, TV shows, or campaigns they starred in, they would always be my family—and that wasn't an act. I looked at my friends who'd made this journey with me to find my family, and I realized they were my family, too: Hana, Martie, Jessica, and most of all, Tom.

Steve Atinsky

is also the author of *Tyler on Prime Time*.
His TV writing credits include the CBS
sitcom *Payne*, Disney's *The Weekenders*, and
World Cup Comedy. He lives in
Santa Monica, California.